Mary Francis Cusack

From Killarney to New York

How Thade Became a Banker

Mary Francis Cusack

From Killarney to New York
How Thade Became a Banker

ISBN/EAN: 9783337121303

Printed in Europe, USA, Canada, Australia, Japan

Cover: Foto ©Andreas Hilbeck / pixelio.de

More available books at **www.hansebooks.com**

FROM

KILLARNEY TO NEW YORK;

OR,

HOW THADE BECAME A BANKER.

BY

SISTER MARY FRANCIS CLARE,

(THE NUN OF KENMARE.)

A Story of Real Life.

FR. PUSTET & CO.,
NEW YORK AND CINCINNATI.

PREFACE.

This tale was written by Sister Mary Francis Clare, the illustrious Nun of Kenmare, at the request of the publisher of McGEE's ILLUSTRATED WEEKLY, to typify an incident in Irish-American life, which, though by no means unusual, can hardly be credited, except by those who have specially devoted their attention to the peculiarities of Irish life, and to its rapid, and generally successful, development under the genial influence of American institutions and customs.

The readers are assured that the main incidents of the tale are drawn from actual life; the moral can be applied by themselves.

New York, 1877.

CONTENTS.

PART FIRST.

PART SECOND.

FROM

Killarney to New York;

OR,

HOW THADE BECAME A BANKER.

CHAPTER I.

TIM O'HALLORAN'S CHOICE.

> "'Tis but a step, down yonder lane,
>   And the little church stands near ;
>   The church where we were wed, Mary,
>   I see its spire from here."
> THE COUNTESS OF GIFFORD.

"Well, I give you your choice, my good man; if you don't care for yourself, care for your boy. The society which I represent will undertake to feed, clothe and educate him the moment you"—the speaker paused. The grey shades of death were settling down in all the awfulness of that time when famine was the slayer of thousands; but there was a fine scorn on the face of the dying man—a scorn which even an angelic being might have expressed if tempted by Lucifer to exchange heaven for earth.

The little flame of life was flickering in the frail socket of humanity, but it flashed up into a blaze as the devil offered his bait.

"And that's your religion," replied honest Tim: "you know I am dying and you want me to face God Almighty with a thundering lie these mountains wouldn't cover," and his trembling finger pointed to the glowing rocks, now purpled with the last rays of the setting sun. "Before the light shines on poor old Ireland again I'll be where there is no sun but Almighty God Himself—glory be to His name!—and His blessed Mother Mary."

"Oh," interrupted the Bible-reader, "if it's the Virgin Mary you're trusting to, I pity you. Why, my good man, will you be so foolish? I promise you to provide for this boy. I promise you to—a—in fact, to make a gentleman of him. But really I must beg of you to consider in your last moments how foolish you are to be putting your trust in a mere woman. Why, how do you know that the blessed Virgin, as you call her, is in heaven?"

"How do I know!" exclaimed the dying man, and for a moment a shade of the rare wit flickered up—the wit that had made Tim O'Halloran famous at fair and pattern for years; "oh, then, sure it's the quare son that would let his mother be in the bad place when he had the power to keep her out of it; and ye say yourselves there's no other place but heaven; so where would the Mother of God be?"

Mr. Blanders was well used to meeting his match in arguments with the Irish peasantry, so he was not particularly disconcerted by Tim's home-thrust. His arguments were golden; but they had not been by any means as effectual as he could have desired. With him it was simply a matter of money. His own religious convictions—if such convictions could be called religious—were simply that one religion is as good as another, but that money was a tangible possession very desirable in this world, whatever it might be in the next. He pitied these poor people in a dull, stupid sort of way, much as a man might pity a poor savage who was offered gold and flung it from him, not knowing its value. He had, indeed, at times, a hazy idea that the Irish knew the value of money very well, but that there was something which they preferred to it, which they called conscience, and which he called obstinacy. One thing, however, was certain—he was bound to get converts. Converts meant money to him. They were prized in the English soul-market at so much per head. At one time, indeed, they were so estimated, but then the head was for the halter, and there was little gain to be had by those who secured the prize. Now times and customs were changed, and the devil was quite ready to accommodate his temptations to the advancement of civilization.

But if the temptation was altered, the cruelty was not lessened. To hang a man out of hand for his religion was merciful compared with the diabolical cruelty of standing beside him with bread and gold while he was dying inch by inch of starvation. The heathen invention of the torture of Tantalus was as a punishment for crime. It remained for the Bible-loving zealots of the nineteenth century to invent another torture for the bodies and souls of the ever-faithful Irish race.

The after-glow had passed; the last ray of sunlight had shot down behind the distant mountains. The cold grey of evening was fast settling into the gloom of night, a little silver streak of light still being visible in the far depths of heaven, and one little clear twinkling star, and still the tempting fiend was there.

The white-winged angels came and went with messages from the Throne, and the Angel of Death hovered very close to the departing athlete. He waited till the victory was perfected, till the crown was won, till the power of soul and conscience had triumphed in the face of the very weakness of death. Moments now were indeed golden, as the sands of life trembled in the hour-glass of time. Moments were being weighed against eternity. Seconds were being counted against centuries. But there was no sign of weakness of soul in all the weakness of body. With every passing moment the angels rejoiced; with every passing moment the demons scowled their hate and despair. And still the tempter-fiend lingered.

That very day Mr. Blanders had received a letter from his English employers, informing him of their extreme disgust at the failure of his mission. They had, they said, treated him with confidence; they had supplied him with unlimited gold, and the result had not been what they expected. The fault clearly must be his, he had not used sufficient efforts to secure converts.

Reasoning from their own point of view these good people were right. They looked on an Irish Catholic very much as they would have looked on a Pagan. They had themselves no choice about religion so long as it was not " Popish." If they had needed wealth, and had been offered it on condition that they should accept any form of opinion, no matter how different from that which they held at the moment, they would not have hesitated in their choice. They could not, then, understand why those " ignorant Irish " could have any choice—why, when they were dying of starvation, they should prefer death to violating their consciences. But, notwithstanding their wonder, the fact remained the same, and they naturally blamed the person whom they employed to effect the attainment of an end which, to them, would have seemed so easy and so desirable.

Mrs. Blanders had read the letter. Mr. Blanders had a very wholesome awe of that estimable individual. Mrs. Blanders had used some very plain and very emphatic language that morning. Mrs. Blanders had advised the partner of her joys and sorrows not to return to the domestic roof-tree until he had "done something," and Mr. Blanders, model husband that he was, had a habit of taking his wife's advice.

The letter which had caused this commotion in the Blanders family had intimated that there was to be a great public meeting in one month from that day, in Exeter Hall, London, and that some thoroughly striking death-bed conversions from the errors of Popery were wanted, and must be forthcoming. It was hard, indeed, that it should be so difficult to procure, when so large a sum of money was offered for it. It seemed, indeed, as if an Irish conscience was the only thing which could not be purchased with English gold, and the desired merchandise was appreciated accordingly.

If a soul could not be purchased, a child could be rescued from

" Popery," and this, at least, ought not to be so difficult of accomplishment.

Mrs. Blanders had some views of her own on this matter, as she said, "if the worst comes to the worst." She had some needy nephews and nieces. Could not one of them be purchased as a sop to the Cerberus of English greed for Catholic souls? One great principle of the society was to ask no questions. Questions were inconvenient. Besides, there was a large staff of officials in England, connected with the society, whose income depended on "something being done," and if a child was snatched as "a brand from the burning," no very particular inquiries would be made as to who the child was.

Mrs. Blanders said to herself "she would see" what could be done. But she had her doubts as to the treatment the poor children received. Some ugly stories of neglect and cruelty had oozed out, and she did not wish to subject any of her own kith and kin to the tender mercies of the soul-destroyers if she could help it. And she was a woman who generally did "help" what she chose to happen.

Mr. Blanders' *forte* was not argument. He had been on the " Home Mission," as his miserable calling was designated, too long to have any doubt about the sincerity and piety of the Irish people. He knew perfectly well that they did not worship the Blessed Virgin, as his English patrons chose to assert. He knew very well that they did not believe that the priest could give them absolution beforehand for the sins they intended to commit. Indeed, the failure of his own mission was one of the best proofs of the blackness of this favorite calumny. Here were men all around him dying of starvation; and if the priest could give them absolution for a future crime, or leave to commit a sin for so much money, why did they die of starvation, or live on a long, lingering agony, when they could so easily have obtained relief?

Tim O'Halloran was not actually dying of starvation—he was dying of famine-fever. He rented a large farm, and had been a prosperous man in his day. When he brought his young wife home, eight years ago, she was the envy of many a lass around

Loch Lein, for she had secured the best match in the barony. The farm was well worked; there were rich, ripening fields of grain, fair meadows, where the Kerry cow chewed the cud and gave rich milk in abundance, as the farm-girl sang to her in the dear old Celtic tongue. The potato had been an abundant crop, and as sweet as Irish potatoes were until the blight came, which seems to have altered even the very nature of the root.

But now all was changed. There were fields of untouched, withered stalks rotting in the winter frost. The kine had long since disappeared from the fair, green meadows. Tim O'Hallo-ran was not the man to store his worldly goods when neighbors and friends were dying for need of them.

A strong man takes long to die. The Scripture-reader still stood his ground. While there was life there was hope. If he could only get one word of assent his purpose would be accom-plished; and if he could not get that word—well, he would see.

Tim O'Halloran turned his dying gaze on the wretched in-truder. Even in his death agony the native courtesy could not forsake him quite.

"I fear you're losing time, sir," he murmured, faintly; "the priest will be here soon, and the priest will care for the boy."

But even as he said the words of hope, the heart of the dying man was sore with apprehensions. His little Thade, his boy, his treasure, his fair-haired lad, with the laughing eye of the mother that was gone, and the winsome way of the wife that never saw the anniversary of her wedding-day.

His little Thade. The boy lay sleeping heavily, wearily, on the same straw on which his father lay dying. Poor little lad! he had been nurse and comforter to his poor father for weeks now, faithful, untiring, with a rare thought and care beyond his years. There was none else to do the little that could be done, save Granny O'Halloran, the aged grandmother, who lived on, as old folks do, through many a hard struggle, when the young fall down and die by the wayside.

Granny was sleeping, too, in an inner room. In the early hours of that day both had realized, for the first time, that father must die. Father James had been there, and said what words he could of comfort, and had given that which was beyond all earthly comfort.

Mr. Blanders started for a moment when he heard the priest was coming. He had had some encounters with that gentleman, in which he had come off second best, and he was not anxious to meet him at such a time and in such a place. But the case was desperate, and the most timid men do desperate deeds when they are between two fires. Mr. Blanders thought of Mrs. Blanders —and waited. Of the father manifestly there was no hope; by some means, fair or foul, he must get the child.

He remembered Thade, and knew what he would be worth, with good food and care. He was a child of much intelligence and of fair presence; he was, in fact, just the very child the society would prize. Mr. Blanders had not decided on any definite plan of action for securing his prey, but he had great faith in waiting.

CHAPTER II.

FATHER JAMES.

Who, in the winter's night,
      Soggarth aroon,
When the cold blast did bite,
      Soggarth aroon,
Came to my cabin door,
And, on my earthen floor,
Knelt by me, sick and poor,
      Soggarth aroon.   BANIM.

A man of stately presence and of a native dignity all his own.
Care, and starvation, and heart-agony had bent the noble form,
had furrowed the open brow, and had added a touching, an almost beseeching pathos to the dignity. How could he see his
children dying of hunger, and not share with them all but what
was necessary to keep the frail scabbard of the body together, so
that the soul might remain to do his Master's work a little longer.

It was the Feast of the Expectation of the Blessed Virgin, and
the whole church was crying out, with her, for the coming Deliv-
erer. He had said mass that morning with trembling hands
and breaking heart. With what tears, with what prayers, he
had cried out for his flock: "Come, O Lord! come and deliver
them." There were worse evils than death to be feared for
them. Happy, indeed, were the dead!

Bands of men had been parading the streets of the neighbor-
ing town the day previous, demanding food and threatening violence. Who could blame them? Yet such open acts of violence were rare, and were more frequently inaugurated by

those who were in comparative comfort than by the patient suf-
ferers who were almost past all power of complaint.

Heartrending scenes had come before him. He had found a
poor mother on the roadside, almost unconscious, with a dead
babe in her arms and a dead child clinging to her skirts. She
was just so far on her road to the poor-house when she fell in-
sensible, and but for the timely arrival of the priest she had died
as she lay.

He had been in a house where comfort and plenty once
reigned, and there he had found the living and the dead lying
together on the same bed of straw and covered with a piece of
old baize that had once been a table-cover. Yet everywhere
amongst these martyr people there was an inconceivable patience,
a supernatural charity, a sanctity altogether divine. And, in
truth, such patience and such charity could not be other than divine, for the grace of God alone could have conferred it.

Father James had administered the last rites of the Church
that morning, as we have said, to Tim O'Halloran. The limbs
that were to move no more on earth were sealed and signed as
the Christian's own possession and property in heaven. Their
last weariness was nearly over; their last pain and ache was well
nigh passed. All the suffering here was soon to meet with its
rich reward on the golden shore.

But Father James had heard Tim's anxious prayer about his
boy. The brave man gladly faced death and bravely suffered
pain, but the great tears rolled down his poor pinched cheeks as
he spoke of Thade.

What was to become of him? The poor old granny had half
lost her wits from age, privation and grief. The neighbors were
scarce able to keep body and soul together, though more than
one of them, with unfailing Irish charity, had offered to take care
of the little lad.

Only the great and good priest could realize how hard Tim's
death-bed trial was. Only God knew how gloriously his faith
triumphed over his fears.

What could the priest say? Thade was one of hundreds of

orphans.   He could do nothing; at best he could but try to see him safe in the poor-house—that miserable substitute for the old monastic houses, where the poor found all their wants supplied by loving and tender hands—the poor-houses, for which the poor have to thank the licentious monster, Henry VIII.—the poor-houses, which even the English Protestant poor so dread that they often die in the utmost misery sooner than face its horrors.

So the only prospect for Thade was as dark as dark could be.

Father James knew, too, that the "soupers" had their eye on him, but he did not know all that we do, or he would have had a sharp lookout after the proceedings of these worthies.

Still he was anxious, and he determined to see O'Halloran that evening again, fearing, indeed, that in the morning he might find only the frail tenement of clay.

He paused for a moment at the door and uttered the Master's blessed salutation, "Peace be to this house and to all who are therein."   Truly there was peace, though it was the peace of conflict.

Mr. Blanders started.

He had not calculated on this encounter, or, if he had, not even his wholesome fear of the partner of his cares would have induced him to remain.

The priest looked at him sternly, and exclaimed:

"Pray, sir, by what right, human or divine, do you dare to intrude on my dying parishioner?"

Mr. Blanders hesitated for a moment, and then, being a bully, as cowards generally are, he replied:

"By what right do you address me thus?"

"By divine right, sir," replied the priest, "and by moral right. By divine right, for this dying man is answerable to God, and not to you, for the faith he professes; and you, *you* would dare to come in his hour of weakness, and try to bribe him (I know your foul devices), to go before his Maker with a lie.   And by moral right I command you to leave this house.   You are here against the will of this good man.   His room is his property as much as your room is yours.   And what would *you* say to the person who forced himself into your presence in your dying moments against your will? Is there one law for the poor and another for the rich?"

Mr. Blanders looked round nervously. He was very anxious to remain. He knew the priest had little time to spare, and what a proud letter he could write to his English employers if he could say that he had defied the priest and remained beside the dying man, "preaching the gospel" to him to his last breath.

" Father!"

The word was breathed so low by the dying man, that it needed, indeed, the ear of a father to catch the sound. But the priest was well used to patient listening, to tender lingering by dying beds when the failing breath gives forth such sounds that only accustomed ears could tell their import.

" Father!"

It was here—it was in the death agony—it was in the supreme moment of human anguish which must come to all, that the blessedness of an office like his can be best understood!

The priest turned quickly to the dying man, and bent over him with a more than ordinary compassion.

"Father, for God's sake drive that devil away. He wants to buy my child; he wants—"

"I know, I understand. He *shall* go, and I promise you, in the name of God, that I will take care of Thade, and that you shall die in peace."

The priest had spoken loud enough for Mr. Blanders to hear him. He now turned to him.

"There is the door, sir, and if you do not leave the house instantly, I will obtain the assistance of the police to expel you from it; and I shall have the place watched to-night, to prevent your further intrusion."

The Scripture-reader thought discretion the better part of valor. There was only one point on which his employer required any special discretion from him. He was particularly desired not to let his proceedings come before the public when there might be any appearance of intrusion.

It was evident, even to the dull comprehension of the "Society for the Conversion of Irish Papists," that it would tell badly indeed if it were known that they forced their Bibles or their agents on those who were unwilling to receive them. It was no matter what was done privately—that was "a triumph of the Gospel."

Marvellous infatuation of heresy and unbelief! These very people, who were forever accusing Catholics of subterfuge and falsehood, put no limit to their own falsehoods and subterfuges, and rejoiced in deeds of the blackest treachery and bribery.*

Then the priest once more gave the dying penitent the last absolution; and after he had called Granny to keep such watch as she could until he could send a protector, he left the cottage sadly.

Tim soon after fell into the heavy stupor of death. Granny watched by him, saying her beads and rocking herself to and fro, in a scarcely less heavy stupor of grief. Poor Granny! It was well, indeed, that her faculties were so dull and blunted by a life of much sorrow and by months of starvation. The morning came, but the straggling beams of the December sun shone on two corpses. Granny had passed away to her long last rest, dying with her beads in her hand.

The lad whom the priest had hoped to have sent to guard the family from the intrusion of soupers had not been able to come. When he arrived in the morning he found there was no living soul to care. Tim O'Halloran and his aged mother were in the keeping of the holy angels.

Little Thade had disappeared.

---

*It is true that much of this curious process of "converting the Irish" has been discarded, but the reader must not for one moment suppose that it is entirely abandoned. At this very moment active proselytizing is going on in some parts of Ireland, and it is carried out with a degree of shameless dishonesty which is scarcely credible. I know of my own personal knowledge instances of this proselytizing. Within the last few weeks a Galway priest has called attention, in the public papers, to a gross case of proselytism—a young girl having been actually detained forcibly in Protestant establishments, where she was kept without food from Holy Thursday until Easter Sunday, because she refused to eat meat. So much for Protestant "liberty of conscience."

CHAPTER III.

HOW THADE WAS LOST AND FOUND.

Wait, my country, and be wise;
Rest and sleep, and thou shalt rise,
And tread down thine enemies.

"Heard the news, father?"

"More deaths, I suppose, Kate; there is little else now."

But Kate's expression of combined amusement and vexation did not indicate so serious a matter.

"Little Thade O'Halloran has disappeared."

"Soupers!" exclaimed Mr. O'Grady, and then he "said a swear."

Excuse him; he was not in the habit of using strong language.

"I saw Father James after mass this morning, and he told me Mick Moriarty had been to Dunn's farm before daybreak. Poor Tim was dead, and Granny O'Halloran was lying dead beside him; but Thade was nowhere to be seen. He called for him and searched for him everywhere."

"It's that confounded Blanders woman," roared irascible Mr. O'Grady, "as sure as—as my name's Miles O'Grady."

"Easy said, father, but who's to prove it?"

"I'll take the law of them; I'll prosecute—I'll expose the whole seed and breed of them, as sure as—"

"My name's Miles O'Grady!" exclaimed a lad of some fourteen summers, who came into the breakfast-room, apparently for the express purpose of continuing his father's sentence.

"You young dog! *you'll* have the law taken of you some day if you haven't more respect for your elders."

But it was no use to scold him, for neither father nor sister could keep anger long with the bright, joyous lad, whose very presence made sunshine in the house.

Mr. Miles O'Grady had been for many years a friend of Tim O'Halloran's. It is true they held very different positions in life. Tim O'Halloran was but a farmer, and, though he was universally respected, he never tried nor desired to raise himself to any higher station. Mr. O'Grady belonged to an old family of high respectability, and in Kerry, where "blood" is held in special honor, his descent counted for much.

His worldly position was not one which, under other circumstances, would have entitled him to hold the position he did. But he was one of the—we had almost said few—Irishmen who, at that period, had the common sense to prefer an honest employment, however humble, to idleness and fancied respectability. He had made acquaintance with Tim O'Halloran when engaged in his occupation of road inspector. Tim's troubles had touched him, for Mr. O'Grady had lost his own wife a few months before his humble friend had suffered a similar affliction.

When Tim found himself dying, he sent a message to the "master," as he always called Mr. O'Grady, but the message had not been received. Messengers were hard to find in those days of dire tribulation, and it not unfrequently happened that the messenger fell himself by the way and died as he fell, or was carried to a fever-shed. Those who once entered those miserable substitutes for home care rarely came forth again to tell the world the tale of suffering and neglect.

"Well, father, have some breakfast, and then you can see Father James, and—"

But Miles O'Grady was not the man to sit down, even to the poor breakfast he allowed himself—for he could not feast while others fasted—while he thought the child of his dead friend was in danger of body or soul. He had scarcely heard his daughter's request; his hat was on, and he was looking in every direction for his stick.

But Miles Junior had abstracted that formidable instrument, in compliance with an ocular hint from his sister.

When Miles O'Grady's blood was up he was apt to use strik-ing arguments, and, in the present instance, a breach of the peace would have been anything but desirable.

For once discretion had the ascendant, and he proceeded to Father James' modest residence, cooler thoughts having suggested this as a wiser proceeding than the general and particular on-slaught which he had meditated on the Blanders family.

Father James could give no information beyond the facts al-ready known. He advised caution, with a very decided misgiv-ing that his advice would be utterly lost on the person on whom it was bestowed.

But he also advised energetic measures, an advice which was scarcely necessary.

Mrs. Blanders was sitting in her parlor, not counting out her money, like the traditional queen in the traditional story, but she was doing what was, perhaps, quite as pleasant. She was count-ing up the probable gain of a rather dirty transaction which had employed her in the early hours of the morning of that day.

Her reverie was interrupted.

"Please, mum, there's a gintleman at the door won't give no name, and wants to see you."

Mrs. Blanders was quite prepared to have any number of gen-tlemen call that morning. She had rather expected the police.

"Show the gentleman in, Ellen," and she hastened to the door herself. It was no policy of hers to keep any one waiting that day.

For once Mr. Miles O'Grady was—as he expressed it himself—"taken aback."

Mrs. Blanders offered him a seat with the utmost politeness, and waited with a masterly assumption of anxiety and deference to hear what he had to say. The consequence was, as she had anticipated, that Mr. Miles O'Grady found it very difficult indeed to know how to begin.

To have "pitched into a fellow head foremost" would have been simple, even if it had not been politic; but to confront an exceedingly civil woman with any remark that was not civil was by no means so easy a proceeding as he had anticipated.

Mr. O'Grady took the seat so politely offered him. He laid his hat on the floor, he took it up, he put it down again; he consulted the inside of it, and for once in his life he wished himself a hundred miles from where he was.

Mrs. Blanders enjoyed the situation, but she was not the woman to allow the little sense of the ridiculous with which she was gifted to interfere with the stern business of life.

She had not the slightest intention of committing herself by speaking. But the silence was broken by an interruption for which neither were prepared. The eldest son of the Blanders family dashed unexpectedly into the room, and not seeing or not heeding the stranger, roared out:

" I say, ma, that boy will make the sign—"

But Mrs. Blanders, though stunned for the moment, was equal to the occasion. A less diplomatic woman would have hustled the boy angrily out of the room, and betrayed herself and her secret, past denial.

Not so the astute " souper's " wife.

For deeds, she merely pressed the foot of her eldest hope in a manner he perfectly understood, and which made him quail not a little for the probable sequel; for words she said: " My dear, where are your manners? You can tell me about your little brother's fancy about these signs another time—free-mason signs," she said, coolly turning to Mr. O'Grady. " These boys of mine have taken a fancy they have found out some great mystery."

Mr. O'Grady was not deceived. He suspected now, more strongly than ever, that Thade O'Halloran was in the house, but even he was well aware that suspicion and proof were very different matters in the eyes of the law.

His courage was restored, however, by the barefaced lie, and he opened his mission, if not with as much tact as he had intended, at least with straightforwardness, which has often a greater success.

" You are aware, no doubt, Mrs. Blanders, that little Thade O'Halloran has disappeared. I called here to inquire—"

But he was not allowed to finish his sentence.

"Really missing, poor boy! how kind of you. But you know he does not belong to our church, and though, of course, we are interested in all our neighbors, you cannot expect us to give you any information on this subject."

"Excuse me, madam; I think your son has given me a little information just now."

"No! really, you don't say so. How rejoiced I shall be if the dear boy is found through our means. Thade O'Halloran—ah, yes, I think I heard yesterday from my husband that the poor father was very ill."

The "dear boy" had left the room in obedience to another silent and expressive caution from his mother, before Mr. O'Grady had spoken.

Mr. O'Grady could scarcely bring himself to say hard words to any woman, and the air of interest and innocence was so well assumed, that a wiser head might have been perplexed how to act.

"Your husband *was* at O'Halloran's last night; he was met there by Father James, and was ordered by him to leave the house. You will be so good as to remember that this can be proved in court if necessary; and, further, it can be proved that the de——, I mean your husband, offered O'Halloran any sum of money if he would give up the boy to him, and offered to make a gentleman of the poor child if he would renounce his faitn. Pretty gentleman, indeed," he muttered to himself.

Something very like a scuffle was heard at this moment on the stairs, and Mrs. Blanders felt assured that the sooner she had her visitor off the premises the better. She knew that to insult his clergyman was the surest way to excite his anger, and if, in his anger, he used threatening language to her, she could the sooner rid herself of his presence.

"Ah, yes, your clergyman, you say; but now excuse me, my dear sir, do you really believe all these priests tell you?" and she smiled a smile of confidential inquiry. "It is all very well for the lower classes, who must be kept in some kind of order; but, you know, a gentleman in your position—"

" Madam, I—"

" Pray, sir, don't misunderstand me. I know you must appear to a—well, to a heretic, as you call me (the noise on the
stairs was becoming louder every moment) to believe all this
folly; but *we* know different," she continued, regardless of gram-
mar, " and in courts of law, at least in England, no one would
believe a priest (she glanced covertly at Mr. O'Grady's expressive countenance and saw stronger words were needed to drive
him out of the house), or these wretched victims of priestcraft."

" If you were a man," exclaimed Mr. O'Grady, with an indig-
nation almost too strong for words; but apparently he thought
words useless or not sufficiently forcible. He stood up, said no
more, walked out of the house with at least an expressed resolve
to have no more to do with women, and evinced his excitement
by a slam of the door which made the house tremble.

A lad passing by, who had not had all the buoyance of youth
crushed out of him by famine, shouted " souper," and added
considerably to Mr. O'Grady's ire.

As he went down the street he met Father James, who was a
man of few words.

" Well, sir?"

" Well, sir," replied Mr. O'Grady, " I saw the woman; and
faith, sir, I'll never face a woman again, as sure as my name's
Miles O'Grady !"

CHAPTER IV.

THE BLANDERS FAMILY AT HOME.

They sold us and scorned us,
Betrayed us and lied;
But we stood up before them
In manhood's full pride.

"It's of no use, Kate; the boy's in the house as sure as my name's—"

Miles O'Grady was very angry. It was too much for his equanimity to have been so ignominiously baffled by a woman, but he was not proof against the look of amusement which his usual form of asseveration had provoked in Kate's sparkling eye.

"What is to be done?" she inquired, without noticing her father's pause. "I suppose you could scarcely bring the case into court."

"Faith, an' it's the divil himself ye might as well bring into coort as the like o' they," exclaimed Mick McGrath, who had been an uninvited listener to the conversation. "Sure, a baker's dozen of the jurymen would be on their side. Glory be to God, but some of the gentry have the wrong cross on them."

"And what were you thinking of?" asked Mr. O'Grady, who suspected Mick had a plan in his head.

"Faith, sir, I was thinking 'of nothing,' as me grandmother said, when—"

But the occasion on which Mick's grandmother made the noteworthy observation was lost to futurity.

Father James had just entered the room unannounced, and a serious consultation followed as to the best course to be pursued under the circumstances.

"We have wealth and power against us, but we have God with us," he said, "and do not for one moment doubt that the father's dying faith will be abundantly rewarded."

"I am certain Mick has some wild scheme in his head," observed Kate; "I only hope it will not make matters worse than they are already."

Mr. O'Grady rose and rang the bell.

"I will caution him—this is no time for acts of imprudence, however well intended.

"Tell Mick he is wanted, and to come at once."

"'Deed, sir," replied the girl, who had answered the summons, "he's just gone out the back way, and he tould me not to keep dinner waitin' for him, for he was goin' to live at the expense ov government, as it was nothin' to do and good pay for it. He would not be 'listin', sure, sir?" she added, half crying, for there had been some little tendernesses between Mick and Kitty.

Mr. O'Grady and Father James rose simultaneously. It was clear Mick was up to something, and he was not exactly the person to conduct difficult and delicate negotiations.

It may be noticed, nevertheless, that mother wit often succeeds where man's wisdom fails; and Pat has a knack of succeeding when he takes any subject to heart.

In the meantime, poor little golden haired Thade was, to use a graphic Irish expression, "supping sorrow."

"You have got the boy now," observed Mr. Blanders with a much of a tone of triumph as he dared to use; "and I should like to know what you are going to do with him."

Mrs. Blanders would have liked a little enlightenment on this subject herself, but she was not going to lessen her prestige by admitting the fact.

"I think when I caught the bird you might cage it," she replied, with a decision proportioned to her own state of mental perplexity. "But it's just like you. How do you expect the society to go on paying you, if you sit all day with your hands before you and do nothing?"

The charge was scarcely true, for Mr. Blanders spent the greater part of the day in personal exercise. He had two good reasons. One was that he was bound "to do good in season and out of season," according to the terms of his agreement with his employers. The other reason was that, though he found a warmer reception than he bargained for when he went on his thankless mission, the warmth of his reception at the domestic hearth was often still more embarrassing.

"Well, Mr. Blanders?"

Mr. Blanders had a happy knack of abstracting himself from exterior affairs when he was not desirous of attending to them. He was at the moment occupied in studying some abstruse problem which appeared to have absorbed itself into a crack in the ceiling.

"Very well, Mr. Blanders, very good, sir; but you need not put on your pious airs with your wife. We had better use plain words and come to a plain understanding." (When Mrs. Blanders elected to use "plain words," Mr. Blanders knew the time for action had arrived, and quailed accordingly.) "Do you intend to support your wife and family, or do you not ? That's what *I* call a plain question, sir; and I want a plain answer."

"Well, really, Liza, you're too—"

"I'm too good for you, sir, if that's what you mean. Here am I losing my time, and every moment precious, waiting the last two hours to hear one word of sense from you."

"I," faintly murmured Mr. Blanders.

"I want no I's, sir; *I've* had enough of you, goodness knows, with your I's. If you'd keep your eyes open, and do something for the good of your family—"

"My dear—"

"I'm not your dear, and I don't want any of your soft solder on me, though goodness knows your're dear enough to me," she muttered, with a grim jocularity which Mr. Blanders had learned to know and respect.

"If you would allow me to speak—"

"Allow you to speak ! Well, Mr. Blanders, that's rather too

much for any poor woman's feelings   Here I am for the last two
hours imploring you to speak.   But never mind, sir, never mind.
Mr. Blanders, was it for this you led me to the hymeneal altar
and made your vows, which are worth about as much as the
poor Papists' that you perjure every day when you make them
swear that they forsake the errors of Popery for those of the
blessed Reformation ?   But I'll say no more, sir."

And Mrs. Blanders subsided, having lost her breath, and really
having nothing more to say.

She seated herself in a large and somewhat ancient easy-chair,
assumed the air of an injured saint and martyr combined, and
put on an attitude of patient attention to any observations which
her husband might make, which would have been quite sufficient
to drive any idea out of the head of any human being subjected
to the process.

When Mrs. Blanders had determined to say no more, her husband was strongly tempted to observe that she had said enough,
and at least to hint at the difficulty of making the observations
she so much desired to hear, but long years of experience had
taught him prudence, and he refrained.

But on this occasion Mr. Blanders was obliged to admit that
his wife's conversation was more desirable than her silence, as he
had not the slightest idea what course to pursue, and he dared not
even hint that his wife was in a similar predicament.

Mrs. Blanders was not slow in pronouncing an opinion when
she had an opinion to give; and the occasions were rare indeed,
in which she did not consider this opinion infallible.

CHAPTER V.

ELLEN MALONEY'S CONVERSION, AS REPORTED BY MRS. BLAND-
ERS.

Faith is the spirit and life in the world.
DE VERE.

"If it's wantin' to see the masther you are, I'm thinkin' I'd better tell the misthress," observed the Blanders' maid-of-all-work, not without a twinkle of humor in her eye.

"Oh, faith, Miss, it's all the same to me, masther or misthress, if they'll do me business handy."

"Maybe it's convarsion you want; it's cheap at the money now, I'm thinkin', for they're few and far between, like the masther's good words," the latter part of the observation being made in a lower key.

Poor Ellen Maloney! She was a "famine orphan," and had been thankful to get a bit and sup in the hard times in return for her services. She was told often enough in the day that she was idle and lazy, and that she did not pay for her keeping. But Ellen listened to it all, and let it pass by like the summer breeze —listened to it as she listened to the denunciations of Popery which greeted her ears periodically.

Ellen was hard working, industrious and cleanly, as Mrs. Blanders knew perfectly well when she took her into her disorderly and thriftless household; but it was not every day that the services of so efficient a girl were to be secured gratis. Ellen had compromised matters in a strange fashion with her uneducated conscience. She had stoutly refused to be converted. She had refused, with equal determination, to attend "family prayers," or the master's church; but she did not go to mass or to her religious duties. She had, indeed, gone to the church and knelt before the altar, with many tears and sobs, "to bid God Al-

mighty good-by" till better times should come, and then went her
way to service, let us hope little knowing the sin she was committing.   It may be supposed that Ellen had very little desire to increase the number of the " mission" proselytes, but if she had
made any active opposition to their increase it would have been
found out, and she was silent.

Ellen's conversion had been paraded with great triumph by her
employers.   Mr. Blanders, under correction of Mrs. Blanders, or,
to speak precisely, at her dictation, had written a touching report.

It was composed with an air of—shall we say assurance or decision ?—which was the result of the undeniable facts that existed,
that Ellen was under their roof, and that she had been a Catholic.
They had few converts, indeed, of whom they could boast so
safely; and they made the most of their advantage.

"I have to report a wonderful instance of the success of our mission, and of our unworthy efforts to spread the Gospel amongst
this benighted people.   Ellen Maloney, a young girl of attractive
appearance and engaging manners, [" What do you want, Ellen ?"
the attractive girl had just opened the door, and rather belied the
description.   "Go away, go away; I cannot be interrupted now.
Where were we, Mr. Blanders?   Really, that girl is a perfect
nuisance—at engaging manners—oh, yes.   Well, you can put
next"] has been brought to see the fearful errors and pagan doc-
trines in which she has been brought up.   When she first saw a
Bible her astonishment was unbounded, and she rapturously
seized the precious volume ["and committed it to the flames,"
muttered Mr. Blanders; "I saw her; she said if she wanted a
Bible she could buy one that was the real thing."]   Since it
came into her possession we have constantly found her poring
over its pages.   ["She can't read two words," soliloquized Mr.
Blanders, but a good deal *sotto voce*.]   She is familiar already
with the names of all the prophets and kings in the old Testa-
ment, [" My dear, you really must try to get her to learn *something*.   If the Rev. Antony Blarney comes down here to inspect
the mission he will certainly question her, and it will be very unpleasant if she cannot answer him properly,"] and we note a
marked improvement in her way of expressing herself on relig-

ious subjects. Our dear children, who have, of course, been well taught Gospel truths, are having a share in the blessed work of her instruction, and have taught her [the eldest hope being present, and hearing himself mentioned inclusively, observes, "Ma, do you know that I heard Ellen teaching Tommy what she said was a text out of the Bible about Mary: 'Hail Mary, full of grace' it was, or something like that, and you said one day it was bad to say it, and how can it be bad if it's in the Bible?" The inquiring mind receives, however, a severe shock in the unpleasant form of a blow on the side of the head, and a recommendation to mind his own business, which—the result of not attending to a similar recommendation on other occasions being vividly remembered—he proceeded to do without further remark] some simple Scripture narratives. We have taken this young person into the house at serious inconvenience to ourselves, but for a work of such importance we are prepared to make every sacrifice, ["Had you not better say something about compensation? Those who live by the Gospel, you know." "I will not say anything about compensation, Mr. Blanders. Hold your tongue and write what you are told."] and, of course, in the painful state of the times and the high prices of provisions, every additional mouth in a household is a heavy additional expense. It was also necessary that we should protect her from the violence of the mob, who, instigated by the priests, were prepared to murder the happy girl. ["My dear, if inquiries are made about this —really, now, you know it is a LITTLE strong." It *was* a little strong, considering that there was not even a substratum of sand on which to build the house of cards. "If inquiries are made, Mr. Blanders, you can refer them to ME, and I hope I shall know how to answer them. You will be so good as to remember that you are writing of what would have happened if we had not given the young person the shelter and protection of our roof." Mr. Blanders thought he was writing (from dictation) of what had happened, but he subsided and continued.] If we have no other fruit to show of our long and weary labors, the conversion of Ellen Maloney would be sufficient to compensate for a large outlay of time and money; but there is no doubt whatever that her conversion will have an immense effect, as the excitement it has caused is prodigious. Largely increased funds may now be entrusted to us with every prospect of a return which will fu.../ repay the outlay. These funds should be supplied as promptly as possible, as I need scarcely call your attention to the fact that unless we act at the moment when the people are ready to receive our words, there will not be the same hope of success."

"Anything more, my dear?"

"I think not. Stay! you had better mention that we do not purpose sending this young girl to the Hawk's Nest at present; she will be perfectly safe here, and my wife will take care that she is not tampered with by her former associates. We have, in fact, thought it well to give her some light occupation in our small family, to occupy her mind, as she cannot be always engaged in Bible lessons. My wife has read some portions of this report for her. Her expressions of gratitude are unbounded, and she would express them herself if we allowed her, only we fear that she would write too strongly about the little we have done for her; and the expense we have had in the matter seems to weigh heavily on her sensitive conscience, though we have assured her that we shall be fully repaid by the kind gentlemen who take such an interest in the benighted Irish race. She is constantly exclaiming: 'Without money and without price—without money and without price;' and contrasting my dear wife's disinterested generosity with the grasping and avaricious spirit of the Church she has left. She assures us that the priest refused to give what they call the rites of the Church to her poor mother, when she was dying of starvation, because she had no money to give him."*

Such is the history of the girl whom we have kept too long in conversation at Mr. Blanders' hall-door.

---

*Such calumnies are circulated even at the present day, to the writer's own knowledge. Soon after the writer of this story was received into the Catholic Church, an educated and liberal-minded Protestant gentleman asked her seriously, and not in any spirit of bigotry or prejudice, how much she paid the priest every time she went to confession. Soupers and so-called converts know perfectly well that these calumnies are base lies, but it answers their purpose to circulate them. If Protestants knew the truth about Catholic teaching there would be many converts; hence the devil has a special and very deep interest in keeping them in ignorance.

CHAPTER VI.

BACK AT THE HALL-DOOR.

> But fixed as fate her altars stand,
> Unchanged, like God, her faith.   DE VERE.

" Well, my good man, what do you want ?"

Mick scratched his head—a not unfrequent, though wholly unaccountable source of information to the Irish mind.

" They're hard times, miss," replied Mick, after a moment's pause.   He did not want to commit himself in a hurry.

Mrs. Blanders began to have some suspicions that there was something in Mick's visit beyond what was apparent on the surface, and acted accordingly.

" You are Mr. O'Grady's man," she said, rather as an assertion than as an inquiry.   There was not a man, woman or child for twenty miles round the country whom she did not know by sight.

" Thrue for ye, miss.   I was his man, anyway; which puts me thinkin' of the English gentleman that asked Jim Murphy to sell him yesterday's paper, and he tould him he couldn't, because he sold it to a Scotchman last week."

Mrs. Blanders was for once fairly perplexed.   What did the man want, and why did he not say what he wanted ?   He did not look poor enough to be purchasable, and he had had a good place with Mr. O'Grady for several years.

It would not do, certainly, to lose a "convert," but it would not do, either, to find herself the victim of some wild scheme of reprisals, such as had often been threatened, and such as she had every reason to apprehend.   Indeed, the depression of the famine year alone had saved her.

It was wit against wit, and caution against caution.

"I think I'd better step inside, miss, if it's plaisin' to you, as Noah said to the little fishes that was swimmin' round the ark."

Mrs. Blanders assented with a sour smile at the man's attempt at wit.   She had, indeed, observed that he looked restlessly up and down the street while this short conversation was being carried on, and that gave her some hope that she had landed a prize.

"Well, now, my good man, what is it you do want?" inquired Mrs. Blanders, with an attempt at amiability which was far more repulsive than her most savage moods.

"Sure, miss, I'm thinkin' of emigratin' to America—after a bit, you know," he added quickly, seeing the information did not appear very acceptable to Mrs. Blanders; "an' I heard tell there was good livin' an' good wages for a poor boy up in Dublin that *wouldn't be too particular about his religion,* and that yourself is the lady that would help a boy to turn an honest penny—and his coat along with it," he muttered to himself.

Mrs. Blanders' mind was quick when business was concerned, and she began to think how she could best utilize the circumstances which, she believed, Providence had thrown in her way.

She mistrusted the man with a woman's keen instinct, and she did not like to be called "miss;" but we must do her the justice to say that she never allowed any personal dislikes or private feelings to interfere with her business.

"But why did you leave Mr. O'Grady?"

"Faith, miss, I dunno, if it wasn't the change-faver came over me.   *He'll* not know where I'm gone, anyway," he continued, but rather as a soliloquy than as an observation addressed to his interrogator.

"Did you know a boy of the O'Hallorans'?"

"Is it a boy of the O'Hallorans', miss?" replied Mick, availing himself of the Celtic propensity to reply to a question by repeating it.

But Mrs. Blanders gave him no assistance.   And, moreover, he was aware that she was watching him very closely.

" A boy of the O'Hallorans', is it, miss? Sure, me hearing's got bad with the potatoes. But maybe," he said, brightening up as if with a sudden and happy inspiration, and with the most charming assumption of a desire to exert his memory to the very utmost, "to oblige the lady "—"maybe, miss, you're meaning the boy that gave the English gentleman the quare answer—the fair-haired chap, you know, that went to Australy last winter. Maybe you heard what he said, miss," he continued, with a desperate effort to get himself out of his entanglement. He looked up at Mrs. Blanders for a moment, but her face was a perfect blank. She meant, at all events, to let him have his say. She could afford to wait. Her plan was formed; and the more she saw of her eccentric visitor, the better, before she developed it.

" It's the way, miss. There was a lot of chaps working up at the church, you mind, there near Muckross domain, an' a lot of English chaps—great swells, you know—with their hi's and their h'ands, comes along, and walks round everything, for all the world as if they were paying God Almighty a compliment for looking at the beauties of nature and art; and then they ups and they goes to them, and one chap gave the wink to another, and the other nudged the next chap, that they'd have some fun out of them Oirish fellows. An' as luck id have it, who should they light on but the boy ov the O'Hallorans'—the devil's luck they had—I mane as them blackguard Saxons, savin' your presence, miss, always has. An' one of them swaggers up to him, puffin' himself out like a Kerry aigle conversin' with a pert sparrow, an' he says, condescendin' like, but with a big sneer on his ugly mouth:

" ' What are you doing, my man ?'

" ' Makin' morthar, sir,' says O'Halloran; ' an' maybe its your eyes you left in England,' he says to himself; but the other gentlemen heerd him, and they signed the Englishman to go on.

" ' And pray, what is this building going to be ?'

" ' A church, sir,' says O'Halloran, an' he workin' away at the morthar, and never a look up he gives at all, at all, but just

shovin' away at what was before him, an' mixin' nicer than ever
the parson did his twelfth tumbler of punch.

" 'Oh, a church—really, now. And pray, a—what a—denomination does it belong to ?'

" 'It doesn't belong to no nomination at all, sir; it's for the
Holy Roman Catholic Church.'

" Then all the other chaps gives a laugh you might hear over
to the aigle's nest, and the chap that was spakin' got quite huffed
like, an' he says:

" 'Then I'm sorry to hear it.'

" 'Faith, sir,' says O'Halloran, an' he spoke up pretty loud,
'an' that's just what the divil says,' an' the other chaps roared
at this. You might a heerd them over beyond the mountains at
Kenmare, let alone at Adrigoole.''

A sense of the ridiculous was not one of Mrs. Blanders' mental
gifts, and she scarcely took in the point of the joke. Indeed,
the cares of a family like hers, and an income held by a very un-
certain tenure, might have dulled the wits of a brighter woman.
Nor did she very much concern herself about the broad hit at her
religion. Her religion, so far as she could be said to have any,
was to provide for her family—to keep her household, husband
included, in order.

But the evening was closing in, and something should be done
with this loquacious individual. For once Mrs. Blanders was
relieved when the door opened and Mr. Blanders entered the
untidy apartment.

"Mornin', your honor,'' said Mike, with an utter and callous
disregard of the time of day.

Mrs. Blanders volunteered an explanation.

"This is a—I believe—a person—a man, in fact—''

"Yes, your honor, I'm a man,'' said Mick, without moving a
muscle.

"Who wants, I think, to a—change—in fact, to improve his
condition.''

"The lady's just puttin' the case neat and elegant, as the
devil said when he put the last nail in the sou— (Lord help you

to hould your tongue for an omadhawn; you'll put your foot in it before you're done, anyhow," observed Mick to himself.) " Never mind, sir; me thoughts is too many for me, as the hin said to the clutch of ducks. It's bettherin' me condition I'm afther, an' your good lady, I'm tould, is the man—(whist, ye villain, and git sinse)—I mean, the woman, to help me."

Mr. Blanders was so frequently told to hold his tongue in private, that he had become rather afraid to let it move in public— at least, when his wife was present.

An exceedingly severe "Well, Mr. Blanders?" brought him to his senses, or rather informed him that he was permitted and ex- pected to make some remark.

" Well, my good man, I am sure we are only too willing to help you. There are a few little conditions as regards religion, and that, but we will make it as easy as possible for you; and my wife—"

" I'll thank you to speak for yourself, Mr. Blanders."

" Oh, well, my dear—"

" Och, sir, the lady and I understands each other—don't we, miss?—and I'm agreein' to all the conditions beforehand, with- out hearing them, an' I'm sure nothin' in life could be fairer. An' look here, miss," and he drew his chair closer, and dropped his voice to a confidential whisper, " about that O'Halloran bey, sure *I* knows what I knows, and mum's the word and silent as the grave. Sure I know the benivolence ov ye that made ye take him that night the father died (God be merciful to his soul and heaven be his bed, amin!) and know ye brought him up to this very house, where ye has him now, and clapped your hand to his mouth when he roared out, not knowing the good ye was doing him; an', faith, I believe ye clapped it to his shoulders pretty smart, too. Och, it was mortial kind ye were to the poor mis- understandin' orphan; faith, it's grateful to ye he ought to be. An' sure I saw the pretty crathur peepin' out of the back windy o' this very house an' I comin', an' he tryin' to make signs to some one in the street beyant, as if the ungrateful little villain did not know what was good for him, an' he pointin' to his arm,

where ye beat him with the stick last night, an' sarved him right,
too; an' the police—''

"Bless my soul!" exclaimed Mr. Blanders.

Mrs. Blanders looked a whole case of pistols at him, to enjoin
silence.

The fact was that Mick had drawn the whole narrative, piece
by piece, from the fertile depths of his own imagination. He
had not seen the child carried away that night; he had not seen
Mrs. Blanders administering personal chastisement to the unhappy
victim of her zeal; and certainly he had not seen the child looking out of the back window as he came in at the front door, for
he was not possessed of Sam Weller's optics.

But he had told his narrative with such an air of confidential
secrecy, with such a calm assumption of knowledge, with such a
kind intention of serving people who were about to confer a benefit on himself, and whom he felt bound in turn to befriend, that
both Mr. and Mrs. Blanders were completely and thoroughly
taken in; and, in their alarm lest the knowledge of what they
had done could be really and legally proved against them, they
quite overlooked Mick's remarkable statement about the peculiar
powers of his organs of vision.

Mr. Blanders was literally trembling. The mention of the police was too much for him. Under ordinary circumstances he had
no fear whatsoever of that respectable body. Whatever their
private opinions might be—and some of them had very strong
private opinions—they were not allowed to express them in public; and however they might have liked to see soupers consigned
to even warmer quarters than a police cell, they were often
under the orders of magistrates who certainly leaned pretty
strongly to the Protestant side.

But here was a case which would be sure to create a very strong
feeling if it was found out; and though Mr. Blanders knew he
would be well backed up with money and patronage, and held
scot-free by the unscrupulous parties for whom he worked, still,
were the case proved, he could hardly carry on his work longer
in Killarney, and it might not answer to have popular feeling run

too high against him; and there were some "boys" in the neighborhood apt to be free with their blackthorns if their ire was roused. The hard times, the utter depression of the people, was all in his favor; still he knew the injured have good memories.

Mrs. Blanders was equal to the occasion. Of course it was all Mr. Blanders' fault. If the day of doom had arrived she would have accused the unhappy man of having precipitated its arrival.

"Ye'd better lave the boy out of this the night," observed Mick, keenly enjoying the sensation he had occasioned. "There's a place, I'm tould, call'd the Hawk's Nest, bekase, I suppose, of the birds that lives in it, an'—"

"The boy must go to Dublin to-night, Mr. Blanders."

That gentleman was not prepared to contradict any observation that his wife made, even had he not lost his mind altogether from sheer fright.

"But, my dear, who is to take him? If either of us leave this, suspicion will follow on—"

"Mr. Blanders, I'll thank you to allow me to speak."

"Ah, thin, but you're the lovin' couple entirely," observed Mick; "when the lady's that devoted she's always privintin' the gintleman ov the throuble ov spakin'."

Mrs. Blanders was far too practical to notice the interruption.

"If your toothache was not so bad, Mr. Blanders—"

"My dear—"

"I said, Mr. Blanders, if your toothache was not so bad, you ought to go up to Dublin yourself, together with this good man and the boy. As it is—well, I'll think about it—you had better come with me;" and Mrs. Blanders, having signed to Mick to remain where he was, and to her husband to follow her, left the room.

"Now, Mr. Blanders, I'll thank you to attend to what I'm going to say. You must go to Dublin with this man. I believe he is in earnest—at least, that he wants to get money, and will make some sacrifices for it; but it would be impossible to trust him with the boy alone. Can I depend on you that you won't make a fool of yourself and spoil the whole business?"

"My dear—"

"You're enough to drive any woman clean crazed—you, the father of a family—God help them !—with no more sense than a teetotum, or—an elephant" (Mrs. Blanders was apt to confuse her metaphors, and wholly regardless of the fact that she had asked Mr. Blanders a question). "Certainly I cannot leave this place with no one but you in it, and of two evils choose the least, which, I must say, in conscience, when you are in it is always the worst. And now I beg you will attend to me and do exactly what I desire, or you need not come to me when you get into trouble again."

CHAPTER VII.

IN THE POLICE COURT.

Oh, thin, Paddy Malone, ye bewildering boy,
Ye're yer father's own jewel, yer mother's own joy.

" Drunk and disorderly—fined five shillings.   Now, then, sir,
look sharp and pay up."

" Is it five shillin's ye mane ?" observed Mick, with a face expressive of utter vacuity; " faith, it's myself that never touched a
whole shillin' since the time I was born, barrin' the one I swal-
lowed when I was a babby, when the doctor—"

" We want none of your talk.   Pay your money and go; five
shillings for you and five for the gentleman that's along with you.
You seem to have got over the drink better than he did, for he
looks drunk and incapable this minute."

" Oh, sure, your honor, sir, you would not be blamin' him; he
has not got his mornin' shut up in that dirty cell all night, an'
he's never himself until the missus comes to his bedside with a
drop to rouse his sowl."

If ever mortal man was in an agony of desperation and despair, that man was John Thomas Blanders.   If ever man realized
that his wife was his better-half, John Thomas Blanders realized
it that day.

Certainly he would have given ten years of his life to have had
her at hand to get him out of the hapless position in which he
found himself.

The result of the private interview between husband and wife
had been a visit from Mr. Blanders to a " medical hall," where

he appeared with his face tied up and considerably swelled, as might be seen by the protuberance of the bandage in which it was swathed.

Having expressed his sufferings by many groans and contortions, he asked for something to ease the pain, and on being provided with a remedy, he said that he hoped there was enough to last him for several days, as he was sure he was in for a bad attack, and Mrs. Blanders did not like sending the servants out of messages.

Now Mr. Blanders was an inoffensive man in general—partly from natural character, and partly in consequence of the severe and excellent training to which he had been subjected since his marriage. But all this availed him little. He was hated for the dirty work he did. Any other sufferer would have been received with sincere expressions of sympathy and condolence; but the only remark elicited by his appearance was a *sotto voce* observation of one shop-boy to another, who wondered if Mrs. Blanders had anything to do with his present distress, and the return observation of the other, that he wondered would it be any harm to put the least taste in life more opium than creosote in the mixture, and give him a sleep that would keep him from doing the devil's work for a day or two.

Whether the opium was put in the "pain killer" or not remains to be proved.

That night Mr. Blanders, Mick and the unhappy Thade O'Halloran set out for Dublin. We cannot boast of any remarkable expedition in our mode of travelling in Ireland at present, but journeys from the Lakes to Dublin are express speed now to what they were then.

Having commenced the farce of the toothache, Mr. Blanders was obliged to keep it up. Indeed, Mick, who had "scented" the whole plot, was glad, for his own reasons, that it should be kept up. His attentions to the unhappy victim of his wife's cleverness would have set a more uneducated man mad; but Mr. Blanders had long gone through a course of constant irritation with the happiest results.

As to Thade, his incessant cries had ceased the moment he saw Mick M'Grath. Children have very keen instincts. Mr. Blanders' honeyed words or Mrs. Blanders' more forcible arguments had alike failed to comfort or subdue him.

Mrs. Blanders was not naturally cruel; but when she found that Thade's cries were likely to create an attraction, even outside the house, which would have been as undesirable as it was unpleasant, she flogged him into silence, if not into submission. When he was told that Mick was going to take him home to father and to granny, his joy was nearly as destructive of the peace of the Blanders household as his grief had been of its safety.

But a word from Mick to "whist," or "to be aisy," was enough.

His first look into Mick's fearless black eyes told him that there was no treachery there, and a "trust me, darlin' !" whispered with a look that the intelligent child was by no means slow to take in, satisfied him that all was right, even if it did not seem so.

Dublin was reached at last, and here it was that Mick had made up his mind to rescue Thade in his own fashion.

Any one who had known what Mr. Blanders suffered in that police court must have pitied him. He dared not open his lips for fear of discovery. He was partly helped by the toothache invention, with which Mike had condoled on his journey, both exteriorly and interiorly, with the kindest expressions of sympathy. It had begun to dawn on him that Mick was playing a game, and he knew pretty well by this time that he was no match for a quick-witted Irishman.

And he had visions of home. Let us say it with all possible tenderness. What man is there of any right feeling, of any refinement, of any conscience, who does not turn fondly to his domestic hearth when cruel fate has torn him from it ?

Mr. Blanders was no exception to the general rule; but his thoughts were exceptional, and they were not pleasant. A triumphant " I told you so !" was mild to the greeting he expected to get when he reached Killarney, minus Thade and minus

Mick. And the unhappy man was literally tongue-tied. He dared not open his lips in explanation or extenuation. His trade was forever ruined if it was discovered that he had been had up before a magistrate on a charge of being drunk and disorderly. It is true, indeed, that his employers were not very particular as to the character of the persons who served. It was a necessity of the case. They got the weeds which the Pope threw out of his garden into the unhappy field where such weeds throve apace. They were obliged to admit that the weeds *were* weeds, but what could they do when they could not get anything else? Clearly, they had to make the best of a bad bargain, and if they found that the bargain was a very bad one indeed, that was their affair. No one had asked them to undertake their dirty work, and stupid as they were, and blinded by their master, the devil, they were perfectly aware that there was no use in any outcry. Any private short-comings of their emissaries and agents were quietly condoned. If they became known to one or two, they were treated compassionately. What else could be expected, they said, from poor ignorant Papists, brought up all their lives in darkness and deceit. They forgot, or they found it convenient to forget, that these same Papists were supposed to be converted. It certainly would have puzzled some of them to have told what they were converted to.

But a public appearance in a police court, " drunk and disorderly"—this, indeed, would have been past forgiveness, or would have necessitated removal of the agent to new quarters. An exposure such as this could scarcely be got over. Mr. Blanders knew it. He might have faced the society, but he could not have faced his wife.

Silence, an assumption of stupidity, and even of the stupor of drunkenness, was his only resource. It must be admitted that Mick entered heartily into his plans, and that he was quite prepared to do all the talking.

"Is it drunk and disorderly, you say? Faith, that chap there," pointing to the unhappy souper, "was a little overcome, I'll not deny it, nor the crathur wouldn't hisself if he was able to

spake to your honor.   But sure you'll forgive him this onct.
Sure it all came of a bad toothache he got payin' rounds at St.
Killian's Lake come last mid-summer, and it hung over him ever
since.   Glory be to God, what some men have to pay for their
sins—I mean their virtues.''

Mr. Blanders groaned audibly.   To be made appear drunk
and incapable was bad enough, but to have himself put down as
guilty of a Popish superstition, and not be able to deny the
charge, was past bearing.

''Ah, thin, is it a heart ye have in ye at all, at all, or maybe
they left it out for some one else whin ye were born.   Don't
ye hear the crathur groanin', your honor's worship, sir ?
Sure it's sorry he is, an' he'll say a whole rosary for you—Holy
Mary an' all the rest—if you let him off.   Sure you never see'd
him afore, an' faith, I'll promise your honor's worship, sir, you'll
never see him again.''

Mr. Blanders assented with another groan.

''Sure it's the bit of a smile I see playin', like a sunbeam, on
your honor's illigant mouth, under the purty bit ov hair you've
got on.''

There was a roar in court, in which his honor heartily joined.

'' There, then, pay your fine directly, and go, sir.   I'll let off
your friend on account of the toothache, and he may thank you
for it.''

Mr. Blanders thought he might.   He owed Mick a good deal
more than he ever expected to repay.

''Is it five shillin', your honor ?''

'' I told you so before.   Make haste—I can't be kept here all
day.''

'' Faith, an' it's meself that always knew me manners to the
quality since Phil O'Rafferty put it into me with the thick end of
an oak-stick.   As for delayin' you, sure—''

''Policeman, take that man out, and give him seven days if
he does not pay that five shillings in ten minutes.''

'' Oh, your honor, you're hard entirely on a poor motherless
boy.   It's the first time he's got into a bit of throuble, and he in

a sthrange counthry entirely. Musha, sir, if ye came down to my place and was overtook a bit, sure it's not hard the gentry 'ud be on ye."

A joke was very well in the way to enliven a dry police case, but the presiding magistrate was getting more than he wanted, and he lost his temper.

" Pay that five shillings and go to —— with you."

" Faith, thin, yer know, I hope I know me manners belther than to be inthrudin' meself on the quality. Sure it's takin' up the room on ye I'd be if I went there."

There was another roar in court, and several custodians of the peace came in from the outside to see " what the row was," while others forgot their dignity so far as to grin broadly.

" Oh, then, bad luck to ye for a five shillin's. It's a dear five shillin's yez are to me," and Mick commenced to feel in every pocket but the right one for the money.

At last he stooped down, and having divested himself of his left shoe and stocking with the utmost coolness produced the money, part from the heel and part from the toe, and counted it down slowly, utterly oblivious of the shouts of laughter that assailed him.

" There's yer dirty five shillin's, and the d—— mend yez with it," he said, as he put down the last crooked sixpence to complete the five shillings, having doled out each piece of money as slowly and as deliberately as he could.

" An' now, your honor, sir, I'll thank you for a resate."

" Pooh, nonsense, man, we don't give receipts here."

" Ah, then, the sorra stir me, or this gentleman, or the little boy 'ill stir out ov this the day." And Mick deposited himself on a seat with an air that indicated it would require at least five policemen to move him.

Mr. Blanders' feelings need scarcely be described, and Thade, with a finger in his mouth and a wisdom beyond his age, clung to his friend and benefactor.

The curiosity of the magistrate was excited.

" Really, you must go out of this, my good man."

"Give me the resate, yer honor, an' I'm gone as quick as ye'd swallow whisky."

"What do you want the receipt for, you fool? Don't you know you won't be taken up on the same charge again?"

"Is it what I want the resate for, yer honor? Well, I'll tell yer honor. Ye'll soon see the raison of it," and Mick settled himself with the air of a man who wants to take his time while telling his story.

"Ye see, yer honor, I'll die some day, glory be to God and have mercy on me sinful sowl, amin. And when I get up to the gates of heaven, there'll be St. Peter hisself there, waitin' for me, an' he'll say, 'It's welcome ye are, Mick M'Grath, but I must ask you a few questions before I let you in;' an' indeed, yer honor, they needs to be particular, for they can't turn a poor boy out when once he gets in

"An' I says, 'With the greatest pleasure, your holiness.'

"An' he says, 'Mick M'Grath, we're glad to see you here, an' we're goin' to let you in, but you'll tell me first did you pay all your debts when you were on earth down below there?"

"An' I'll say, 'In coorse I did, your holiness, every one of them.'

"An' he'll say to me, 'Well, if you did, Mick M'Grath, where are your resates?'

"An' I'll say to him, 'Here's every one of them, your holiness, barrin' one.'

"An' he'll say to me, 'Mick M'Grath, it's sorry I am to be keepin' a fine boy like you out in the cowld, along with them Protestants that didn't know any better, but I can't let you in till you bring that one, an' ye must go an' get it for us.'

"Sure a mighty ill-convanient thing it would be for me *to be goin' down below* lookin' for your honor to get me resate."

CHAPTER VIII.

THREE LETTERS.

Famine slaughtered where plenty reigned,
Starved mothers died ere their babes were born,
And—merciful Father of the forlorn !—
Men dared to say 'twas by Thee ordained.

P. O'C. Mac L.

" MADAME: I write to inform you that a person was brought to our hospital last night who, as far as we can ascertain, is your husband. He is quite unable to give any account of himself. In fact, he has evidently met with rather rough treatment, as we have reason to think, from a mob.

" He was brought here, however, by a respectable-looking countryman, who told us that he took pity on him, as he was from the same county as himself. Indeed this good man seemed quite devoted to your husband (if we are right in our supposition that our patient is your husband). The man, whom, no doubt, you will know, as he expressed himself very warmly about you, [Mrs. Blanders expressed *herself* rather warmly at this point] seemed quite broken-hearted at the condition to which, I regret to say, your husband was reduced. He told him repeatedly to cheer up, that he would be a friend to him, that he would be sure to write and tell the mistress all particulars. This assurance appeared to distress your husband greatly, as, no doubt, he feared the effect it might have on you. We hasten, however, to assure you that there is nothing really dangerous the matter, Mrs. Souper (we conclude this is the correct name, as Mr. Michael M'Grath assured us expressly that it was). Mr. Souper has hope-lessly broken his left arm, fractured the right leg, and there is a rather deep incised wound on the forehead; he is, moreover, bruised in several places rather severely; but with time, and the judicious treatment for which this hospital is famous, he will, no doubt, recover.

"It is now more than a week since he was left here by his friend, Mr. M'Grath, who promised to write you full particulars. As, however, we have not heard from you since, and as Mr. M'Grath has not called here again, as he promised, we think it better to write fully.

"Mr. M'Grath informed us that he had come up to Dublin in company with your husband and an orphan boy whom they were trying to rescue from some proselytizers. He said you expressed great concern for the poor boy, and had urged your husband to come up to Dublin with him, though he was far from well. You will be glad to hear, he said, that the boy was quite safe from further persecution.

"If we understood him correctly, he said that your husband was apt at times to take a little more than he could bear, never being a very strong man, and that this was the reason why you asked him to go up to Dublin with him. It seems that he had taken too much, notwithstanding Mr. M'Grath's watchfulness, on the evening of the day that he was brought to us, and that, though he never uses bad language at other times, he has an unfortunate propensity for doing so when he is at all overcome by drink. On this evening, unfortunately, he first cursed King William and then cursed the Pope, and was taken before the magistrate, and fined for being drunk and disorderly. Mr. M'Grath said he paid the fine for him out of his own pocket. Indeed through the whole affair he appears to have acted with the utmost delicacy and consideration. But after Mr. Souper was released, he became worse than before, and created another row in a low public house, where he was maltreated by two parties; as a consequence of his cursing both Catholics and Protestants, both parties were offended.

"We are under the apprehension now that his head *may* be slightly injured, but pray do not make yourself uneasy on this subject. Our reason for thinking so is his very strange manner. He refuses to reply to any questions, he will not give his religious denomination, and he keeps his head constantly covered in a way which suggests a morbid fear of observation. This is especially noticeable when the Protestant chaplain makes his visit. Indeed, he has done his utmost to induce Mr. Souper to converse with him, but he finds it impossible to get even a word from him or to see his face. Under all the circumstances, though, we again repeat, there is no danger. We think it better that you should come up to Dublin, if possible, at once. We have less hesitation in making this request, as Mr. M'Grath informed us that you are in affluent circumstances, and that you devote your time and money to works of charity amongst your fellow Catholics.

" I beg to subscribe myself, madame, with profound respect,

" Your obedient servant,

"JOHN MULLINS,

" *House-Steward at the —— Hospital, Dublin.*"

"P. S.—You will pardon me, I am sure, for writing so familiarly, but Mr. M'Grath said so much of your amicability and disinterested benevolence, that I feel already as if I had the honor of your acquaintance.

"P. S.—In compliance with Mr. M'Grath's direction, I address the letter to Mrs. Blanders, for Mrs. Souper, New Street, Killarney. He says that Mrs. Blanders is very intimate with you—in fact, quite a second self—and that by addressing you thus the shock will be broken to you."

Mrs. Blanders' feelings on receipt of this communication will scarcely bear description. The catastrophe was so appalling and so wholly unexpected, that she was simply stunned into silence.

But she was a woman of action. As soon as she could think, her first thought was, what was to be done? She had not one moment's doubt as to what course Mick had thought fit to pursue. Having disposed of Mr. Blanders, he would certainly return to Killarney with the child, and what an exposure there would be.   Clearly the place would be far too hot for her and for her hapless husband.   Their missionary work was done there, at all events.   What was left but to shake the dust from her feet, and to go where the Gospel message would be received with a little more success and gratitude?

Mrs. Blanders remained in profound reflection for ten minutes, and then she wrote a letter.

"To the Secretary of the Society for the Conversion of the Irish Nation,

" REVEREND SIR:—The long years of arduous work which we have spent amongst an ungrateful people have at last been crowned with a wonderful success, but at the cost of great suffering to my devoted and zealous husband.   It is well that we have not sought any temporal gain, or we should have been sadly disappointed.   We have, indeed, not counted the cost.   Our house has been open at all hours of the day and night to those who desired to hear the Gospel message; and my husband has been travelling, in season and out of season, through the surrounding districts with the Word of Life.   We have distributed gratuitously the 2,000 Bibles you sent us, and we hope when the Irish-speaking population of this district has learned to read and speak English, they will be perused with great attention, and that the precious seed which we have sown will bear fruit at last in this unfruitful soil.

"A great opportunity of saving a poor, benighted soul has occurred here lately.   You may be assured, and can assure the society, that we took care it should not be lost.

" One of the most respectable farmers in this district was dying of famine fever, and my husband scarcely left him in his last hours, administering with the tenderest care to his spiritual and temporal comforts.   The poor man was overjoyed to have his company, but the priest, as usual in such cases, interfered, and drove my husband away.   Late at night the dying man was, however, most anxious that his child should be rescued from the hands of the priest.*   He entreated my husband to take the boy home,

---

*Such lies are frequently told in the reports of the societies.

and you may be assured we know our duty to the society by which we are employed too well to refuse such a request. The difficulty was, however, how to secure the poor little child. But the long experience of my husband, and his fertility in resources, suggested an expedient.

"On entering very late at night, we found the father was dead, and the boy, who is about seven years of age, was sleeping by his side. I went with my husband, as on such an occasion I could not listen to the promptings of flesh and blood, or consider the severity of the weather, though just recovering from severe illness caught in the discharge of duty. We took the poor boy so quietly that he did not awaken until the following morning, when he found himself in a comfortable bed in our house, and was soon reconciled to the change. But we were obliged to get him out of Killarney as quick as possible, as my husband could not prove that the father had given the child up to him, having no witness present, and of course the priest would have sworn that the man died a good Catholic. Your society knows how prudent we have been, and how we have always avoided anything that could compromise us in the eyes of the public, or bring the mission into difficulties, unless when some very serious interest was at stake, when, of course, we would do our duty regardless of consequences from which we know the society has sufficient power to protect us. We got the boy up to Dublin last night, but unfortunately my husband lost him in a crowd, and having attempted to address a few words of Scriptural instruction (very unwisely, I must add, but his zeal has no limit) to some sailors, he was set on by them and severely injured. It will be some weeks before he will be able again to travel, and the expense for medical attendance and lodging in a private house will be very heavy. But we are sure your society will amply compensate him for what he has suffered in your service. One partial failure this time will insure success on the next occasion, and, as the boy was actually brought to Dublin by my husband, we expect to be paid the usual grant of £50 for saving a child, besides expenses. The boy's name can be entered on the books of the society, but prudence will require that his own name should not be entered. You might put him down as Michael Murphy, aged thirteen, and, for the same reason, it is well to alter the age. He may be entered, also, as sent to America, to save him from the persecution he would have to undergo if he remained in this country.

"Hoping to have a remittance from you at your earliest convenience, to cover expenses, I remain,

Reverend Sir, etc., etc.,

SOPHIA BLANDERS.

"P. S.—I think we had better leave Killarney as soon as possible. We could do more good now in any other place."

Mrs. Blanders read her composition over several times very carefully, and felt satisfied with the result. She knew that questions would not be asked nor very minute inquiries made as to the truth of her statement. In fact, the whole business required a great deal of "confidence" and a very large amount of make-believe on the part of those principally concerned, and when all were equally interested in multiplying statistics, there was no question about the process by which they were made up.

Mrs. Blanders received her money in due course, with warm commendation for her humanity and devotion. She went up to Dublin as soon as possible, and after she had relieved her feelings and done her duty by informing her husband that he was a fool, she subsided.

Matters had turned out better than she had expected; in fact, almost as well as if poor Thade had been in the Hawk's Nest.

Her husband knew so well what his wife's opinion of him was, that he could bear to hear it reiterated without much concern. He was, in fact, both thankful and surprised to find that he escaped so easily.

LETTER NO. 3.

To MR. MYLES O'GRADY, ESQ.,

In the street near me Mother's house,

Killarney,

August the one, 18—

RESPECTFUL SIR: I write these few lines, hopin' it will find you as well as it leaves me at present, barrin' the yellow faver, for which we're in quaranted, which was brought on boord in a hin-coop, which a boy of the Sullivans' came in from New York, looking for the chickens which his mother promised to send him from the ould country; but there was none of them left, for we had an awful storm, glory be to God, at sea, an' went part way down to the bottom in the ocean, but come up again quite right, praise be to his holy name; and the hins were drowned dead, and there was not one left above wather, that the poor boy cried a pailful of tears; but sure where was the use an' the distance so great?

"I axed the captain—a civil-spoken little gentleman enough for an Englishman—how many miles it was to land the time we was going down the sea, an' he said two Irish miles was equal to three ov theirs, an' that shortened the road wonderful. Honored sir, I never was let land on the pier, but I am writin' this by a boy that is a wonderful scollard, entirely, entirely. Sure he's got the finest character yez ever seed, an' his testimonials, as he calls the bits iv paper he has by him, is signed by all the clargy in Ireland, and more than all the gentry. Dear, dear, what it is to have the book-larnin'! I wish me mother had sent me to school with a stick, an' I'd be doin' this meself, so ye'd know it was me own writin'. 'Deed and sure, respectful sir, I'm told by some ov the boys here that this chap's testimonials is superior to his character, an' no wonder, with all the priests to the fore. Well, well, I hope it's takin' the shine out ov them Yankees he'll be yet, for the honor and glory of ould Ireland.

"It's a quare place entirely, this. Would yez believe it, now, respectful sir, but the hoight ov the quality live in brown stone houses, an' they say they're illigant entirely; but, faith, a brown mud cabin would do the likes of me, if I had the bit of ground round it, an' no landlord to pay rent to but meself.

"Honorable sir, will you tell the ould mother that it's not forgettin' her I'll be; but we can't go yet on land, for there's nothin' to walk on but the wather, or they wouldn't keep me long here. They say it's twenty-one days we'll be in it, which is equal to three weeks at home. Bad luck to them, with their quare ways of countin', that puts a poor boy out entirely. Ye may tell the poor woman that I'll send her a present soon. As I know she likes what's nate and plain, an' not showy, I've bought a nice bright orange-colored kerchief, that she'll look like a rale lady in goin' to Mass, as it will have been twice over the says, as the captain's boy brought it from one of the men in the East Indies, where they don't want any clothes, and so can part with them chape. Lord save us all, what a quare place the world is entirely, that the people can't even wear their clothin' itself. They tells me here they have got a wonderful new invention that'll do away with the letters entirely; and sure it would be a blessin' to the young chaps that won't want to learn them, for all the writin' 'ill be done by touchin' bits ov wires, and they say it is done by the quare thing up in the sky which, glory be to God, I never saw but once, and then it was me brother saw it, for I was too long wakening up when he called me.

" They tell me, too, there's a place up North where the sun never sets part of the time and never rises the other part, and sure I told them it's a pity they can't persuade the gentleman to do it more regular. But don't think, respectful sir, that I got a fool since I left Killarney, and believe them; faith, no sir—your honor, I mane—I took good care to let them know they need not put a *comether* on me with their lies, an' I afther doin' that souper woman. Oh, thin, your honor, only it's afraid I am I'd be kilt dead entirely and put into prison afther to reflect on it by the peelers, but I'd have liked to have stay'd at home to see the fun out. An' that puts me in mind that I've come to the beginning of me letther, which I forgot before. The boy that's writin' this says this should have come first; but sure if he takes a clane piece of paper and puts this end at the beginning, it'll be all the same, as the chaps is comin' in and out with nothin' to do, an' all helpin' each other while we're doin' this writin', an' makin' remarks on every word I say, which is makin' his hand shake so that I'm sure his own mother would not know the writin', poor woman, though I don't suppose she couid read it much easier if she did.

"Well, of all the desateful sarpints, since Eve and the Garden of Eden, that woman's the worst. The lies she told about that boy would fill one of her own soup-kettles over and over, and it would not be short measure 'ud be in it, either. Sure I thought of her when we were going to be drowned comin' over in the sea, and the man kept turning the wheel to keep the vessel up; but we prayed to the Holy Virgin and the blessed Mother of God, that never refused the prayer of a poor Irish boy, that died dead for the true religion over and over thousands of years ago, before her and her soup kettles were even heard of. But the boy that's noldin' the pen says his hand is aching with listening to me and putting down all this, bad manners to him. I believe if it was a faction fight he was in, his hand would not ache on him so aisy.

"Anyway, I must hurry up now, for I hear we are just going to land, and I want to get round to the stores, for that's the quare name they have for the shops here, an' I suppose it's be-cause they have such a lot of things stored up in them, an' not like Kitty Brady's little general shop in Killarney, where they never had anything particular except a few dip candles and a pipe or two. I'm told there's plenty of employment to be had for any-body, an' I'm goin' round to all the places to ask if they have got room for a vacancy, and that I'm agreeable to take it.

"Hopin', respectful sir, we'll meet in that land of eternal glory, where the worm never dies and the fire is never quenched,

Your obedient servant,

MICK M'GRATH.

"An' for the boy that wrote for me, if it 'ud be plasin' to your honor, sir, to tell his mother that he's from Killarney, and that he'll write to her when he gets on land.

"P.S.—I hear now it's not the yellow faver that we had at all, at all, that it's further up the country, and is, as you may say, a pleasure comin'. It's a bill of health we've been in. I'm sure with their bills an' their stores, it's hard to know the manin' of a word they say. Sure I thought it was when a man was sick the doctor sent in a bill. Faith, an' it's fine times they must have here if they can send in a bill for health as well as for sickness; but poor Ireland was always an oppressed country. The heat is awful, an' I'm sartain sure if I live here much longer that I'll die an' the half of me 'ill be melted away, and then one-half of me 'ill be looking for the other half at the day of judgment in the streets of New York, Amin, Glory be to God; but I suppose the holy angels 'ill know which of us is which, an' won't be mixin' up one with the other, and not of the true religion.

"P.P.S.—Here I am at the end and haven't said the beginning yet. Sure I suppose Thade tould you all he could, the cra. thur, the night I put him in at the hall door, and went right off to America that minute. Take care of that boy, your worship. He'll be a credit to ould Ireland yet. I know you'll take him an' give him a bit o' larnin', and don't let him forget poor Mick, an' tell Ellen I'll sind for her."

PART II.

***

CHAPTER I.

WHERE AM I GOING?

But this my black despair, when thou wert dying
No breath of prayer did waft thy soul to heaven.

B. J. H.

"Oh, my God, my God, where am I going?"

"Hush, my dear, you'll only make yourself worse."

But still she cried and moaned, as only the dying can cry and moan, "Oh, my God, my God, where am I going?"

A pitiful sight it was, indeed, and one to make the angels weep.

Even her husband's love could not soothe her now. She knew it could not pass with her over the terrible barrier between life and death.

But one short year ago she had come, a gay and thoughtless bride, to her husband's splendid mansion in —— Avenue, New York.

Death! What had she to do with death, when wedding congratulations were still ringing in her ears, and wedding presents were all untouched by time?

Death! What had she to do with death, when her young life was just beginning, when the young blood was bounding joyously through her veins, and the tenderest love of a noble man was all her own?

Death! If the idea had crossed her mind at all, it was only to think that it might come to others, not, certainly, to her. For the young have a strange way of thinking death impossible for themselves, but possible for all others.

Death ! She was face to face with it now, *and she knew it.*

A man face to face with a savage animal—with a roaring lion—with a raging tiger, would have had less fear. The possibility, however vague, of escape—the chance, however slight, of defeating his enemy—the peril, so great as to rouse every nerve, to demand every thought for the one purpose of self-help—this would have lessened, if it would not altogether have deadened fear.

But she was face to face with death, *and she knew it.*

Scant time to prepare for that which would need a life-time of preparation, and pitiful ignorance of how to prepare.

There was no reprieve. In a few hours all would be over. Every alleviation that wealth and love could give was hers; but these very alleviations seemed a cruel mockery now. What could wealth do for her? Nothing. If all the gold and all the jewels and all the wealth of the whole world could have been brought to her and laid at her feet, it would have been just as much use or comfort to her now as a stone lying on the roadside.

She looked round the room, with its sumptuous arrangements, its costly mirrors, its silken hangings, its golden ornaments, and she smiled to herself a smile of utter misery. What use was all this to her now? As much use to her, and no more, as one of the brown stones of which her house was built. And yet she knew there were people who envied her this brown stone house with all its costly appurtenances.

Love ! What good could that do her now, except to add a deeper pang to the last agony ?

Ah ! if love could have saved her, she would have been saved.

Her husband sat moaning out his anguish at the foot of her bed. Her baby had been taken away—she did not even notice it.

There was something *now* which claimed her for its own—something which demanded all her strength. For one who had been, as men call it, nursed in the lap of affluence—for one who had been an idol at home, and a yet greater idol, if possible, in her new home—there was scarce a trace of selfishness in her character. Loving and lovable, gentle and tender, true and faithful, caring less than most young girls for the attractions of society or for her own attractions—she only wanted one thing; and in that supreme hour all that she possessed could not compensate for that want or purchase it for her.

She could not be satisfied with platitudes. A man in momentary danger of death will not thank you for assurances that he *may* not be in such peril, after all.

Her husband had tried to comfort her, at first, in this way; but he saw it was useless. What was he to say? What was he to do? He! why he had not been in any place of worship six times in his life, and then he went, not to worship God, nor to pray for pardon for his sins—no, it was to hear some popular preacher, a man who, living himself a life that even his friends could scarcely call moral, yet dared to take the name of the Living God in vain by preaching a Christianity of his own invention.

He was not the man to help the soul in that terrible hour. The husband would not allow him inside his house, though he would pass an hour listening to his preaching as he would pass an hour at the opera or the theatre.

There are stern realities in life which need something more than words.

She only noticed the baby once. It was June, and the summer roses were giving out all their fragrance—such fragance, at least, as they can give in a crowded city like New York. A few fresh buds, bathed with dew, were lying on her bed. She took one in her hand, and with a look of unutterable love and anguish, she said:

"Call her Rosaline."

There was no need of words. He understood.

A fanciful name—a poetical name; not one to remind her of a saint or of holy things. Not one to help her to prepare in any way for the death which must come to her also.

Again the poor dying girl moaned, "Oh, my God, my God!

where am I going?" She knew the name of God, and that was nearly all she knew of religion. Time and eternity seemed to have changed places in the minds of those who had educated her. Everything in this world was treated as if it was to be eternal, as if there could not be any change, as if it were all to go on forever.

Eternity, if thought of at all, was treated as some vague, indefinite, wholly unimportant matter. It did not seem worth a thought. Certainly no serious thoughts were given to it.

But now this girl-bride was face to face with eternity, and it seemed to her as if she should never have thought of anything else.

How she would have envied Tim O'Halloran's death-bed! How willingly now would she have changed places with the poor, famine-starved Irish peasant, whom once she had been taught to despise! What would she not have given for one little minute of their glorious faith, their sublime hope, their perfect charity!

But as we live, so we shall die, one and all. We have had time enough given us to arrange for the future; if we have not availed ourselves of the time, the fault is our own.

Mr. Maxwell did not know what to do. How could he offer the consolations his poor wife needed so much, when he was so utterly ignorant of their source? He had literally been without God in the world. How was He to be found now, who had never been sought until now? It is true, indeed, that mercy is promised even at the last moment, that there is hope for all; but it is too often forgotten that we have it in our power to put ourselves in such a condition as to be beyond the reach of mercy willfully and premeditatedly.

Even the heathens believe that there is a God, and worship Him—ignorantly, it is true—yet they do worship. But what shall we say of those who bear the name of Christians, and yet who never bend their knees to their Maker, never offer Him the homage of their prayers or of their praises, who never utter His holy name except to blaspheme it?

And yet Mr and Mrs. Maxwell were not of this class. They

were what the world calls good, well-meaning people. They did no evil, indeed, to any one—they were merciful as those who know not God may be merciful—to every one except themselves.

But what a terrible exception. Let us suppose that we have been the means of saving the whole world by our prayers, and tears, and penances, yet that our own souls were lost! That, at the great Day of Doom, we should see thousands entering heaven, and should be the means of their having done so, and yet should find ourselves condemned to hell. What consolation would it give us, that they had been saved while we had been lost—that they should listen to the songs of the angels, while we groaned in anguish at the curses of the demons?

Mr. Maxwell did not feel as his wife felt. He felt *for* her, certainly, as men do feel when the light of their life is about to be extinguished—as men feel when they think the world can never again afford them a moment's happiness.

But we cannot compare the feelings of a man on the point of perishing from a violent death with the feelings of one who merely looks on at danger.

Mr. Maxwell was not face to face with death. *He* had not to ask himself, "Where am I going?" He was not in the position of one whose life is counted by hours, if not by minutes.

But his wife, his bride, his love, to her had come the agony of death—in no dulling stupor of insensibility, which sends so many souls unconscious to their doom—souls who might have prepared for it before this came, but did not.

To her had come the agony of death—not as it comes to many, in such anguish that pain almost deadens every sense, so that the soul is unable to realize the terror that is coming—no; her life was ebbing away, yet her soul was quite able to note each change, each advance of the fell destroyer, Death.

The saints who have lain dying—who have cried out in transports of adoring joy, "When shall I be in heaven?"—they have lived for heaven, and now they reap their reward in a foretaste of its joy.

The wicked have lived for hell.

It is as awful as it is true.

The wicked have lived for hell, and now they have a foretaste of what is prepared for them—of what they have chosen.

And the poor, dying girl had lived for hell. She knew it now, alas! too late.

She had her choice, as every mortal has, and she had chosen. Her choice was none the less deliberate because it was not made with any loud expressions of blasphemy or defying of God. She had simply and quietly passed God by. She could not profess ignorance of Him. She said in a general way that God had been very good to her; but even this goodness had not touched her heart—had not made her think of Him. She was simply indif-ferent—but her indifference was sin, and she knew it now.

She did not think—that would have been excuse enough once; but she was face to face with realities now, and she knew she dared not make such excuses. She knew now that it was her duty to have thought. She knew now that God had given her a mind and an intellect that she might use it for Him, and she had used it for the devil.

What had her thoughts been occupied with? The world, its cares and pleasures, herself—with precisely those very things which God had expressly forbidden. Certainly she had not broken those laws of God which were the laws of her country. This was all the world asked from her. She must not offend against the code of morals which the world has condescended to sanction. There must be an outside observance of some kind of morality and order. It is the devil's reluctant tribute to Al-mighty God. The world, for its own sake, is obliged to enforce some rule—a proof, were proof needed, how necessary rule is.

CHAPTER II.

BLOOD-GUILTINESS.

The guilt of another! God help that soul
That bears such a burden of sin and fears,
One only art can wipe out the crime—
A life-long penance of pain and tears.

M. F. C.

" Where is Kathleen ?"

Mr. Maxwell thought, and with apparent reason, that his wife's mind was wandering.

" Kathleen ?"

" Yes."

But there seemed no sign of wandering, though the voice had grown perceptibly weaker.

If she had asked for her baby, or for some near and dear friend, he would not have been surprised; but Kathleen was an Irish servant—the only Irish servant, indeed, in that large establishment. Her place was an humble one; but she was a smart girl, and would soon rise to a far better position.

" My darling, what can you want with Kathleen ?"

" She knows something about religion, I am sure; they say all these Irish servants do. Their priests do something for them when they are dying. Oh, Willie, Willie!" she cried, and wrung her poor hands in anguish, " it is hard to die, it is hard to die !"

" My darling, what should you be afraid of? You never did any harm."

" I am afraid of God."

" But they say He is merciful. Surely, surely He cannot be hard on you."

" He is merciful; but if the Bible is true, He is merciful only to those who have served Him faithfully. What have I ever done for Him ?"

True; what had she done for God ? Nothing. And she knew it now, when she was face to face with death.

Nothing !

We do something for those whom we love. We are never weary of doing for them. Our hearts are full of desire to please them, to surprise them with some act of gratitude, of affection.

"If you love Me, keep My commands." Which of God's commands had she kept ? Not one of them. Had she ever done one single act of her life for the love of God ? No. She had simply never thought of Him. Had she feared him ? No. She was simply indifferent.

Once, indeed, a little thought of fear, of holy fear, had come.

She had gone to that most marvellous of all Nature's marvels, the Falls of Niagara. As she gazed awe-stricken upon the rushing mass of waters, a thought of God had come into her heart. The flashing lights, the rainbow clouds, the thunder of the waters, brought to her recollection some words she had seen long before, it seemed—some words of the great glory of the Eternal One, who sits above the mighty waters, who pours them forth from the hollows of His hands—of thunders and lightnings surrounding the throne of the great Creator—of the whisperings of music upon the harps of a virgin throng who follow the Lamb everywhere.

The voice of God spoke to her through the voice of Nature, and in the mighty falling of the cataract waters she heard the whisper:

God !

She knew God had spoken. For a moment her heart was touched.

It was but for a moment. God had given His grace freely. She had done nothing—nothing whatever to merit it. He had given His grace kindly, oh, how kindly! She had never given him one loving thought.

God, if we may say so, had set a device for her, a plan to win her; but she was not to be won.

The supreme moment passed—passed forever!

Mr. Maxwell sent for the servant. He would have gone himself for a priest that moment if his wife had asked him. He loved her far too dearly, far too unselfishly, to hesitate for a moment in complying with any desire which she might express.

But before he allowed the girl to enter the room, he spoke to her outside the door.

"Your mistress is dying," he said; "she is greatly distressed in her mind. If you can do anything to help her or comfort—"

"Oh, sir, what can I do?"

"I thought—she thinks—you are a Catholic."

It seemed as if, in saying that, he had said all that need be said. He did not know why Kathleen trembled. He did not know why she had become so suddenly and so ghastly pale. He attributed her hesitation to timidity, and said:

"This is no time to think of yourself, girl. If you can help my dying wife, for God's sake do;" and he forced her into the room.

"Kathleen, oh, Kathleen, help me!"

Already the eyes, once so extolled for their beauty, were glazing in death. It seemed, indeed, as if terror of the future kept her still lingering here. The little vitality left was sustained by this strange stimulant. She could not die, it seemed, in this terror—in this darkness—in this awful dread.

Kathleen flung herself on her knees by her dying mistress. She scarcely knew her. There were so many helps in that great mansion, that one more or less mattered little. It was not a house where *souls* were counted, as souls should be in all Christian households.

"Oh, ma'am, what can I do?"

Again she wailed out: "I thought you were a Catholic. I thought Catholics could do something for the dying."

As the moments passed and no answer came, the shadow of an unutterable despair settled down upon her.

" Oh, ma'am, I was a Catholic—I am—but it is years since I practiced my religion."

Years since she practiced her religion, and time is counted only by years, which are but as minutes in the great spaces of eternity !

" Let me go for the priest," she cried.

" Oh, no—it is too late now—too late ! too late !"

It was too late.

Before priest could arrive, the hour for her departure would be sounded upon the dial of time.   Each moment, as it passed them, was worth a prince's ransom.   A prince's ransom !   It is a poor comparison to make.   All the wealth of India, all the wealth of all the world put together, could not delay the supreme moment.

Faster and faster the minutes seemed to fly, and Kathleen suffered a death-agony with her dying mistress.   She realized now to the full what she had done.   She, with full light, with full knowledge of her religion, without an excuse before God and man, had flung away her glorious birthright as a Catholic, as a member of that faith which even infidels have admitted to be the grandest religion the world has ever known.

Unhappy, miserable girl !   Already her sins had found her out.   Happily for her, she had time for repentance; but to her dying hour she would go bearing about the bitter burden of BLOOD-GUILTINESS.

She was guilty of spiritual murder, *and she knew it.*

If she had been faithful to the teaching of the holy faith in which she had been born, baptized and educated, what might she not have done for the soul of that dying woman ?   How she might have comforted her, and taught her, and helped to win her over to receive the ministration of God's holy Church !

The girl knew her religion very well.   She knew if there was immediate danger of death, and that there was not time to get a priest, that she should have herself administered conditional bap-

tism, and taught her dying mistress how to make an act of contri-
tion for all her sins.

And then this poor soul might have gone hopefully to God.

Protestant baptism is so carelessly administered, principally because it is considered a mere ceremony of no moment, that, awful
as it is to say so, it is to be feared that the greater number of
Protestants are unbaptized, and we know that those who die
without holy baptism will never see God's blessed face in heaven.

This poor dying woman, then, is deprived—not by ignorant
Protestants, who deserve more pity than blame, but by a Catholic—of the greatest grace which mortal can desire.

Kathleen knew full well what she ought to do; but the paraly-
sis of mortal sin was on her, and she hesitated till the time for
action was past.

Then, indeed, when death had claimed its prey, she cried out,
with an exceeding loud and bitter cry, "Oh, my mistress, my
mistress!"

But what tears or cries could help now? The time of probation
had passed—the hour of judgment had come.   Time enough had
been given both to mistress and maid.   Time enough to prepare
for eternity.   Time enough, intellect enough, opportunity enough.
What excuse could either mistress or maid offer, when called to
account before the judgment-seat of God?

Kathleen had come to New York some few years before, as
many another Irish girl had come, with little thought of anything
except to advance herself in the world.

The sudden change from the regular habits of home life had
not improved her. She was her own mistress now, and gloried
in a freedom which was to work her ruin.

She went to Mass regularly at first, and every Saturday for a few
weeks she intended to go to confession. We all know the old
proverb about the way to hell. It is, indeed, paved with good
intentions.

No girl says to herself deliberately, "I will go to hell." But,
alas! how many boys and girls choose *deliberately* to walk in the
path that leads to it, straight and direct.

Here is the fatal error. Here is the terrible danger. And yet how awful is the blindness of those who precipitate themselves into these snares.

A man who is walking along a road which ends in a dangerous pit-fall is told often and often where he is going. He will not say deliberately that he is going to walk into destruction. Far from it. He will assure you that he is very well able to take care of himself; but those who went the road before know well the folly of his rash confidence. If he continue on that road, he *must* end by precipitating himself into the yawning chasm from which he can never be rescued.

And what is the danger of temporal death, compared with the danger of eternal damnation!

Kathleen had been the envy of many Irish girls in New York, in consequence of her success in obtaining such a good situation and such high wages. She really had done well for herself in a worldly point of view, and this was to her credit, if she had not neglected what was far more important.

But worldly prosperity is always dangerous. It needs a double watchfulness on the part of those who attain it. They have, indeed, need to look well to the salvation of their souls, lest, having gained all in this world, they should lose all in the next.

At first Kathleen had the best possible desires and intentions. She would have been indignant and furious with any one who had even suggested that *she* would become a partial apostate from her faith. What! could any one suppose that she would turn from the religion of old Ireland—from the faith for which thousands of her forefathers had bled and died !

And let it be remembered how a traitor is execrated in Ireland —that a man who outrages his country, or who turns traitor on his countrymen, is ever shunned and hated and despised, and justly so. But what should we say of those who become traitors to their God and their faith, not from any dire temptation or distress, but only because they fear a few words of ridicule from some fellow creature, or in the foolish hope of temporal advancement ?

Kathleen had lost grace by neglecting to attend to her religious duties after her arrival in New York, and she was therefore an easy prey to the tempter. Her fellow-servants, who knew nothing about religion, ridiculed, as the ignorant will always do; and she who was once wise became a fool—not for God's sake, but to please the devil.

What was she to get in exchange? She was giving away eternal gain to win temporal loss; for in truth, no one ever respects a man or woman who is not true to their religion.

She was risking her eternal salvation for what? Because a few words of ridicule had met her ears now and then.

Poor fool! poor fool! What king would fling away his crown and descend from his royal throne, because an envious few make a mock of his royalty?

And yet do we not too often find that those who should be faithful to their God, that those who may wear a royal crown, and who have a royal throne prepared for them in heaven, will fling it all aside because they fear some little word which will be forgotten almost as soon as it is uttered—because they are fools enough to listen to the sneers or persuasions of some bad companions, who will laugh at them in the end for their folly in being so easily led!

Ridicule may, for a time, be the portion of those who are steadfast to their religious principles; but in the end faithfulness is always respected, and will surely have honor in this world as well as in the next.

BLOOD-GUILTINESS!

Kathleen shuddered as she thought of it. She had been guilty of spiritual murder, so far as it was in her power.

If a mother, looking at her little babe in its cradle, could see the hangman's halter round its neck—could know that this child would one day imbrue its hand in the blood of a fellow-creature, what would be her anguish, what would be her horror! Day and night she would be haunted by the terrible thought—day and night the horrible future would be before her.

Do not let us forget that it is far more awful to kill the soul than to kill the body. Let us sometimes think how fearful will be the agony, the anguish of those who are guilty of spiritual murder.

Let Irish Catholics, especially, think of the work God has given them—the glorious mission of converting the world. From north to south, from east to west, the Irish Catholic has gone forth on his glorious mission. It is the Irish Catholic who builds the churches, who supports the schools; yes, who give priests for the mission in every English-speaking country in the world.

Woe to those who fail in the great work or hinder it ! Woe to the Irish man or woman who neglects his religious duties, who is ashamed of his religion, who has upon him the sin of blood-guiltiness, since he does his best, according to the world's example, to help those around him to lose their souls, while, if he remained faithful to God, he might save not only his own soul, but the souls of those with whom he associates.

CHAPTER III.

THADE.

"A sunny, laughing Irish boy,
His father's pride, his mother's joy."

"Thade is growing up a fine lad, father."

It was Kate O'Grady who spoke, and what she said could not
be contradicted.

Since the night on which Mick had put the poor child inside
Mr. O'Grady's door, with a piece of paper pinned to his frock,
and inscribed in Mick's "printed characters," the nearest ap-
proach he could make to penmanship, Thade had been a general favorite.

The inscription ran thus:

"Here's Thade, your honor, sir; an' if that desavin' blackguard comes afther him, tell her to go to her master, the ——."

Mrs. Blanders, as we have seen already, had her own plans,
and was not disposed in the very least to interfere with Thade
and his friends. She had quite sufficient sense to know when a
case was hopeless, and sufficient mother-wit to keep herself out of
trouble that would not pay.

So Mrs. Blanders and her husband had absconded. In fact,
for many reasons, they had discovered that a foreign mission
would be more agreeable to their taste; and even with all the
liberality of the "Society for the Conversion of the Irish from the
Errors of Popery to those of the Protestant Religion," it would be
far more remunerative.

To Mr. Blanders' great amazement and his still greater joy,

Mrs. Blanders had simply relieved her feelings on their first meeting by the emphatic utterance of the words:

"You're a fool!"

Mr. Blanders had been told this so often, that he had at last come to accept the assertion as incontrovertible, or as an established fact which it was useless to dispute.

She then informed him that she had arranged with the Society for the Conversion of the Cannibals.

Mr. Blanders demurred. He had a habit of taking things *au pied de la lettre*, and really believed that for once his wife had lost her wits.

On venturing a slight remonstrance, accompanied by a timid suggestion that he would, on the whole, prefer dying a natural death, he was silenced very peremptorily.

"Did I say you were going to live with the cannibals or near them? Thank God, if you were born a fool, I was not. Of course we must send home lists of converts; but I think we've done that before now," she added, not without a touch of scorn; but whether for the credulity of her employers, or for her own humiliation in being obliged to earn her living by such mendacious proceedings, we are unable to tell. "But," she continued, "remember that there can be no inquiries made as to what takes place thousands of miles from here, and that converts can be got there a good deal cheaper and with far less trouble than in Ireland; while there is a fine opening for commerce; and, I am told, on good authority, a fortune can be realized in a very short time and with very little trouble. That done, I suppose we can come home and attend to our own business."

Thade had been sent regularly to school, and had got a fair education. In those days common sense ruled in this matter, and an unfortunate school-boy of twelve or fourteen was not obliged to learn as many "ologies" as a professor. Good reading, good penmanship and good arithmetic were considered the essentials, and were taught and respected accordingly.

Nor was Thade ungrateful. He poured forth all the warm-hearted devotion of his race on "the master" and the young ladies of the family; but Mr. Tom, the eldest son of Mr. O'Grady, was the special object of his attention and devotion. For him he would have laid down his life freely at a moment's notice, and Mr. Tom's career and success in life was of far more moment and consideration in his eyes than his own.

It was with no little pride that he entered the breakfast-room on a bright day in the early part of July, 18—, and handed Mr. Tom a letter, with the observation:

"Official, sir."

It was official, and contained an appointment which Mr. Tom had most ardently coveted. Warm congratulations were poured out on him by father and sisters, for he was idolized by his family, as only sons are apt to be, especially when they have been the last pledge of a mother's affection. Mrs. O'Grady had long lain with her fathers in the beautiful old abbey church-yard, once the home of the Franciscan fathers, at Muckross, near the Lakes of Killarney.

Thade lingered, as a privileged domestic, to enjoy the scene, and to offer his own share in the congratulations.

"Yes, it's all right, my boy," said Mr. O'Grady; "only that Father Mathew put the spell on me against a drop of whisky, I would tell you to drink the young master's health."

Thade, happily for himself, had never tasted anything stronger than water, and had not the slightest desire to do so. Would to God that the Irish peasant would save his children from all fear of future misery, by taking the simple precaution of not allowing them the opportunity of acquiring a taste for the poison, which does the work of the devil better than he could do it himself.

"You'll not want the horse now, sir?"

"True for you, Thade, and you will have your heart's desire."

It must be admitted that to be the possessor of a horse was the highest flight of Thade's ambition. He had done well at school, and Mr. O'Grady was now thinking of binding him to a trade, or even of placing him in an office.

Let us have a glance at him as he stands in the bright morning sunlight, in the pleasant homely parlor. Tall for his age, lithe, well-fashioned, with more muscle than most boys of his years—a very pleasant picture to look on. Constant exposure to weather had slightly tanned a complexion which otherwise would have been rather fair for his sex. A certain look of gravity—which, however, was only a look—gave somewhat of an intellectual turn to his whole appearance and manner; and he was a boy of more than ordinary ability. He looked, in fact, more like a gentleman's son than a peasant lad, and his constant association with the family of his patron had tended not a little to promote and keep up a natural refinement.

But the boy's chief attraction was in the honest glance of his light clear blue eye. Truth and fun sparkled from those truly Celtic orbs; and one might feel certain that, whatever mischief Thade got into, he would give a truthful account of his exploits, no matter what blame might be the consequence of an honest avowal of his faults.

His chief fault was a somewhat reckless disposition: not the recklessness of an ungoverned temper—certainly not the recklessness of vice. It was rather the result of a natural impetuosity of character common to our race, which too often leads the violent or reckless to do deeds of daring defiance, under the mistaken impression that they are doing deeds of true bravery.

Such a disposition has all the materials of an intellectual character, and needs only a guiding hand and a wise director to develop into a character of more than ordinary merit.

After " Mr. Tom," Miss Kate was the shrine at which Thade offered his homage. Miss Kate had, indeed, taken no ordinary care of the orphan boy. She had taught him more than he could ever have learned in any school. It was she who had prepared him for his first confession and for his first communion, and wisely and well had she fulfilled her charge. There was not a boy, gentle or simple, in all the country around, who answered the bishop better when the dread ordeal of examination in catechism had to be passed.

Certainly Thade knew his duty well—his duty to God and

his duty to his neighbor. If he failed hereafter, it was not for want of knowledge.

His was a happy preparation for the great battle of life—a battle the result of which is so momentous, that they are indeed accountable and guilty who fail to prepare their children for it.

Here, in one little moment, the most awful decision may be made. Here, in a passing second of time, we may win or lose a battle that will make our future eternal gain or loss. And surely, if it is disgraceful to find ourselves on the losing side in an earthly conflict, through our own cowardice or ignorance, it is an infinitely worse disgrace to be conquered when we are fighting for our eternal interests.

Kate O'Grady was as light and joyous a girl as ever trod the shores of Killarney's beautiful lakes. But she was none the less grave when gravity was a duty—none the less wise when wisdom was needed in her household cares.

And so happy Thade had the very best guidance that an orphan boy could have. He had imparted to him knowledge of the truest kind; for if we do not know our duty, how can we fulfill it ? The soldier who goes into battle without any knowledge of the tactics of war, would meet with certain defeat. The Christian who goes into the battle of life without knowing what he must do in order to be on the winning side, is, indeed, in a critical position. And, besides knowledge, he must have exercised his art, he must have used his arms, he must have tried his metal.

And so, from his early years, Thade was taught both to know, and to put in practice what he knew. Hence, when the hour of temptation came, terrible as it was, he was well prepared.

CHAPTER IV.

NOT ALL SMOOTH WATER.

He is brave who dares to do
The right, however fools may taunt.

"You're a coward!"

"I'm not."

"But I say you are, and I dare you to do it."

Now there is nothing a fine, high-spirited boy hates so much as to be called a coward, and Thade was no exception to the general rule. Unquestionably, boys have not always right ideas on the subject of courage, and with all Thade's careful training, there was a weak point there. Many a boy has simply become a coward because he did not choose to bear the reputation of being one—a reputation not given him by the good and wise, but by those who were cowards of the basest kind themselves.

"You know I am not a coward. Who saved you when you upset the boat on the lakes last summer?"

It was a fact, indeed. Thade had gone on a boating expedition with some other lads during the preceding summer. They had upset the boat, as boys will do in their wild fun, with little thought as to the probable consequences of their rash act.

Death seemed certain. Only one could swim—(what fatality is it which prevents boys from learning so useful and desirable an accomplishment?)—and that one boy was Thade. The instinct of self-preservation is strong, and it might certainly have been supposed that Thade would have saved himself, and left the lads, whom he had often warned, to their fate.

But Thade was brave, truly brave, and he had that self-sacrificing generosity which invariably accompanies such a disposition. The idea of saving himself never seemed to have occurred to him; and yet he was as young and life was quite as dear to him as to any of his companions.

The capsizing of the boat had flung all the boys into the water. Thade seized the nearest boy, who was evidently unable to keep himself afloat, called out to the other two to cling to the capsized boat, and had landed his prize, as we may well call it, and returned for another, before help was sent in answer to the shouts of the terrified boys.

Clearly Thade was not a coward; but he was afraid of doing wrong—afraid as only a good and brave boy may be. The coward trembles before the petty tyranny of a companion, or the idle taunts of a fool. The brave boy fears God, because God is his Maker, his Master, and his Lord. He fears because he loves, for divine fear is but another form of perfect charity.

So the boys did ill to taunt Thade with being a coward, and they were half ashamed of themselves when the taunt was uttered. But boys often act with little thought, and do harm to themselves and others the extent of which they are very far from realizing. Moreover, boys do not like to be baffled in their plans, good or bad, and, human nature being what it is, the boys were determined that Thade should do as they desired. They were not going to be disappointed, nor did they like to own that Thade was right and they were wrong, though they knew it perfectly well. Alas! how much pride has had to do with human sin since the devil dared Eve to disobey her Maker.

"You know I am not a coward, boys, but I don't like to—to—"

Thade hesitated. We did not say he was quite perfect—who is? He did not like to do wrong, but he had not quite moral courage enough to say so. You see, after all, moral courage is a much higher gift than physical courage, and it is far less common.

You will see a man do deeds of the utmost daring which only

require great physical courage. You will see men peril their lives again and again to save a comrade or gain a point of vantage on the battle-field. Yet these same men will stay away from Mass, will neglect their religious duties, even if a little word of ridicule is said of them—sometimes when no such word is said, and when they only fear it.

Are they brave men? I think not; they are the veriest cowards.

They will get great applause—*and they know it*—for their deeds of physical daring; they will meet with gibes and contempt—for awhile, at least—if they have the moral courage to practice their religion.

It is a bad choice. The applause of men passes away with the breath that utters it: the applause of God and the holy angels will be proclaimed before the whole world at the Day of Judgment, and will last forever.

"Oh, he's afraid of Miss Kate."

They wanted to touch Thade in a sore point. No boy likes to own that he is under any sort of control to a woman. They forget how Jesus obeyed Mary in the holy house of Nazareth. They forget that the men who have distinguished themselves most in after life were generally those who, when boys, were the most obedient to their mothers.

"I'm not afraid of Miss Kate or of Miss any one else," replied Thade, with a toss of his head which showed that the shafts of ridicule were telling.

"Oh, you're not afraid, ov coorse," said James Murphy, "we all know that; but I don't see why you can't have a bit of divarsion, as well as another boy."

"Don't you see he's the makin's of a gentleman in him?" said impudent Joe Flanagan. "He won't demean himself to run races with the like of us."

All of which was exceedingly galling to Thade's high spirit, as it was intended to be.

"Oh, come, Thade," said the very boy he had saved from drowning; "don't let the chaps have that to throw in your face. Who'll be the wiser? I suppose you know how to ride a race as well as to swim a mile."

It was a well-told shot, and very worthy of its suggester, the devil.

It seemed to poor Thade that all his honor and glory and fame as a runner and a swimmer was melting away, and would soon disappear from human gaze, if he did not in some way distinguish himself as an equestrian. Poor Thade ! he was not the first who lost his well-earned fame by attempting what was beyond his power.

Now, Brian Boru, Mr. Tom's horse, was an object of Thade's special affection. He had the sole charge of the splendid and spirited animal—much too spirited, Mr. O'Grady thought, even for his son; for what call had he with a racer? But Mr. Tom thought otherwise. What young man of two-and-twenty ever admitted that his horse was too spirited ? If any boy ever did make such an admission, he certainly was not an Irishman.

Certainly Thade would far rather have suffered any injury himself, no matter how serious, than to have allowed any harm to happen to the horse, and the condition of his equine charge proved that his devotion was practical.

Both Mr. O'Grady and Tom had charged Thade strictly never to ride Brian Boru beyond a walk. They had their reasons, and wise ones. Thade was a high-spirited boy, impulsive and mis-chievous, though not in the worst sense of the word. They quite anticipated that he would be tempted by other lads to run races when he took the horse to water morning and evening at the lakes, and they both assumed that a strict prohibition would be his best safeguard.

Of course Thade promised, and most certainly he intended to keep his promise. But Thade was mortal.

"Come on, boys," he said, when he could stand the bantering no longer, or thought he could not. He did not know how greatly he would have enhanced his reputation for courage if he had withstood—how he would have secured for himself a charac-ter for firmness which would have saved him from future as-saults, if he had only acted according to the dictates of his con-science.

" I thought you would not like to be a 'Molly,'" shouted Joe.

Even then Thade hesitated.   Was it for this absurd taunt he was going to disobey the best master boy ever had ?

The race was run, when Thade found himself flying along the road at a more rapid pace than he had ever thought possible, his brain wildly excited, as a spirited boy's always will be when he rides a noble horse.

He dashed wildly on, leaving his companions far behind.   He won the race, certainly, but at what a price !   The noble animal, finding his rider had no control over him, swerved hither and thither in his mad career.   At last he dashed against a huge boulder at the side of the road, flung Thade off on his head, and the poor brute lay himself on the roadside an apparent helpless mass of suffering.

When Thade came to himself he found he was not much hurt, he was only stunned; but the noble animal which had met with such a careless, reckless rider, was hopelessly, and, for all he knew, fatally injured.

CHAPTER V.

THE TEMPTER AGAIN.

Mother of Jesus, Lady dear,
  Help the sinful and suffering here;
Listen to the sinner's cry—
  Aid those who live and those who die.

"Here comes Thade and Brian Boru," exclaimed Tom.

"Rather late," observed Mr. O'Grady, without looking up from the paper, which he usually perused at his breakfast.

But Kate O'Grady's quick eye had seen that though Thade and Brian Boru were unquestionably passing the house, it was not in the usual fashion.

Thade, who had a fine taste for music, might generally be heard whistling some lively and popular air in the intervals of addressing affectionate observations to the horse. He would pass the windows on his way to the stables with as quick a trot and as jaunty an air as was consistent with orders in regard to his charge and his own ideas of respect to his master.

But this morning Thade certainly was not riding; he was not whistling; he was not even giving the passing glance that he always gave.

Clearly something was seriously wrong; but whether with Thade or Brian Boru, Kate O'Grady could not tell. She knew her father's quick temper—the temper that was so difficult to rouse, and so awful when it was aroused—and she trembled for her favorite, feeling quite sure that harm had come to him or his charge, knowing well that her father, in his anger, might not stop to discriminate between an accident and a negligence or a serious fault.

She looked at Tom, who appeared not to have any misgivings. If there was wrong, clearly, the sooner it was remedied, the better; and the more quickly her father was made aware of it, the better.

" Shall you ever have finished breakfast?" she said, rising from table, with an appearance of gaiety she was far from feeling.

" Oh, I'm done," and Tom rose also. " I will go and have a look at Brian Boru."

" I will go with you," said Kate, who was lingering at the door, and had noticed that her father was too much absorbed in the paper he was reading to be likely to follow them.

" Tom, I'm afraid something has happened to the horse or to Thade. I noticed them as they passed the window, and was afraid my father would see it."

" Pooh, nonsense, Kate; you're always fearing things," observed Tom, with a young brother's usual self-assurance and self-confidence. *He* had not noticed anything wrong, so there could not be anything to notice.

" Well, I hope you are right; but—"

They had just reached the stable door, and a pitiable sight met their eyes. Brian Boru was manifestly hopelessly lamed, covered with dust and dirt, and how far otherwise injured none could tell without careful examination. Thade lay on the ground in an agony of grief and despair.

Tom went to the horse at once, too completely overcome to utter a single word.

Kate went to the prostrate boy, who, whatever might have happened, seemed to her woman's heart an object of the deepest pity.

" Thade ! "

Thade turned his head a little when he heard the voice of his young mistress. It was the first time he had ever feared to look in her face, but he dared not do so now.

Tom was recovering the shock which had stunned him at first, and he seized the boy by the collar, shook him roughly, and set him on his feet.

"Gently, gently!" exclaimed Kate, afraid lest interference might do harm, and yet dreading the rising anger in Tom's eyes.

"Gently, indeed! I don't think the young scoundrel has been very gentle with my horse." Another shake; and indeed Tom was justified in his anger. "Here is the finest racer in Killarney, that my father gave such a sum of money for not a month ago, as far as I can see hopelessly lamed, and you talk of being gentle! Wait till my father comes," and Tom turned in haste to look for him.

"Oh, stay, Tom, stay—at least wait till we hear more—till we know how it happened."

It must be admitted that Tom was forbearing when he complied with her request.

"Thade, how has this happened?"

No answer.

"Thade, what have you done?"

No answer.

"Come, Thade, this will never do. I have taught you to be a truthful boy, and you know your Blessed Mother in heaven will not love you if you are not honest in word and deed. The truth must be known sooner or later; be a man, and tell it now yourself."

With many sobs and tears and groans of real heart-felt anguish, Thade told his story. Told how he had been tempted by the boys, until, believing that they only wanted "a bit of fun," he had yielded to the temptation, and blamed himself bitterly. There was no excuse; he knew it well.

He had been fully instructed, had advantages which these poor lads were never likely to possess. He had friends such as they could never hope to have. He had an education which at that day was rare indeed. And yet for a few mocking words he had disobeyed the most express commands of his employer—of his good master. He had disobeyed commands given again and again, and there could be no possible excuse for his fault.

But we are all too apt, both in blaming ourselves and in blaming others, to look more at the consequences of a fault than at the fault itself.

It was so in this case. If Thade had not injured his master's property so seriously (Tom declared the horse would never be fit to run again), he would have thought very little of the act of disobedience. It is often well for us that the consequences of our faults are so serious, for then we view them very differently to what we might do if it were otherwise.

Yet parents are too often cruelly unjust to their children in such matters. They will punish with severity, almost with cruelty, some fault which has caused them serious loss and inconvenience, though it may not have been culpable in itself; while they will pass over some serious matter which has been a grave offense against God, because it has not touched their own feelings or interests.

Mr. O'Grady was so absorbed in his paper, that it was some time before he rose from the table; but when he did he recollect-ed Kate's remark about the horse, and though he attached but little importance to it, he thought he might as well go to the stable and see for himself if anything was wrong.

The sight that met his gaze when he arrived there held him spell-bound for a moment, but only for a moment. His temper, as we know, was hasty. The condition of the horse spoke for itself. Tom's attitude of utter despair, Thade's tear-swollen and guilty face, and Kate's attitude of fear and anxiety.

" You young scoundrel, you have destroyed the horse !" ex-claimed Mr. O'Grady.

A riding-whip lay at hand. It was but a moment to seize it, and to inflict a shower of blows on Thade's shoulders. He certainly deserved a flogging, but, to his credit be it said, he felt the shame of his conduct far more than any corporal punishment, however severe. But the sharp pain seemed to bring him to himself. Before this he had been stunned and stupid. Now he could no longer bear to face the master whom he had so grievously offended, and with one wild cry he fled out of the stable and into the street.

Mr. O'Grady's anger cooled almost as soon as it had risen, but he did not follow Thade. The boy would come back, he thought, no doubt, in the evening—where else had he to go?—and the horse needed immediate attention.

Thade, after running wildly for some time he knew not whither, came to a sudden pause. Where was he to go? What was he to do with himself? In his then frame of mind, he thought he could never face his master again. He had made but few acquaintances, he had no near relations, nor did he wish any one to see him in his present plight.

The doors of the cathedral were open, as the doors of a Catholic church are ever open to receive the wanderer and the weary, and with little thought of prayer or God at the moment, Thade went in and flung himself prostrate on the ground, in a dark corner, in all the stupor of grief.

The day passed on, but he took no note of time. Evening came, but still he did not stir. At last a care-taker noticed him lying on the ground, and told him he could not remain there for. the night.

He rose up slowly to leave the church, and then a circumstance happened which changed the whole course of his life.

CHAPTER VI.

ROSALINE.

Airy, fairy Rosaline,
Gentle, loving Rosaline,
Beauty gains more grace from you—
Kind and grateful, good and true.

"Well, really, Mr. Maxwell, I wonder you have allowed that child to be brought up a Roman Catholic. It will certainly be an injury to her prospects in life, though the heiress of the firm of Maxwell & Co. may well defy adventitious circumstances."

"I will not do otherwise. It was my poor wife's last request that her child should be brought up with some definite religious views.' And Mr. Maxwell, even as he spoke, seemed to recall the terrible death-bed scene, and to shudder at the recollection.

He was not a Catholic himself. His wife's death had made an ineffaceable impression on him; but it was a human impression, nothing more, and, as such, it had little effect on his life.

"I suppose that Irish nurse of hers is the source of the evil, as the Irish seem to be of all the evils in the country, if we are to believe men like—"

"I know nothing of the Irish, and care nothing for them," replied Mr. Maxwell; "but I would certainly like to see Ireland, and half think of crossing the ocean this summer. Will you come?"

But before this momentous question is answered, we must glance at the history of the little Rosaline, and at the faithful Irish nurse to whom she owed so much.

Kathleen's remorse, after the death of her mistress, was something terrible; but happily it was not the remorse of despair. For a little while, indeed, the demon, who was unwilling to let go his prey, fought a battle with her which seemed likely to end on the side of eternal loss.

She was too thoroughly aware of the consequence of her own neglect of her religious duties to deceive herself on that subject. She had witnessed the terrors of a death-bed unilluminated by even one gleam of hope. She knew perfectly well how this death-bed could have been made one of peace and consolation. It is true, indeed, that those who neglect God in their days of health and happiness, cannot expect Him to work miracles for them in their hour of death and despair. So far the unhappy young mother had only to thank herself for her misery. But Kathleen knew that she would have to answer at the judgment seat of God for the sins which had caused her to fail in the moment when she might have given such blessed help to a dying fellow-creature.

Her first thought was despair, or, rather, this was her first temptation. It is a subtle temptation—a temptation too often used successfully; and what does the tempter care whether he destroys his victims by one snare or another ?

It was no use, she thought, to repent now, after all the evils she had done—as if the good and merciful God, by allowing her to live so long, was not actually calling her to repentance. She was ashamed to go to the priest after having remained away so many years from the sacraments; but happily she thought how much more ashamed she would be at the Day of Judgment, if she did not now make her peace with God, and obtain pardon in the way which He himself has appointed.

But grace triumphed. With many groans and many tears, Kathleen went with her sad story to the priest, and she found not only pardon, but peace and hope. Often in after life would she quote her own example to some poor girl who had remained perhaps for years absent from the sacraments. She would tell her how she had feared and dreaded to confess her sin, how cleverly the devil had tried to discourage her by this means, when all other means had failed; how long she had hesitated, and how she had trembled at the very thought of entering the confessional.

But, as we have said, grace triumphed. The devil's ways are ways of cruelty and misery. God's ways are ways of peace and joy. The devil knew very well what peace and rest she would find in the Sacrament of Penance, and so he did his evil best to keep her from it.

There was one duty for her now, and that was the duty of reparation. It is a duty which even our own conscience must tell us that God will demand from us. It is a duty which even the world requires. If we have done evil, we must atone for the evil; if we have done injury to others, we must, by all means in our power, repair that injury.

Unhappily this duty is too often neglected, too seldom considered as it should be; and if the reparation is not made here, most certainly it will have to be made hereafter.

Kathleen's first thought was to beg admittance into some convent as a lay sister, where she might, by prayer and penance, make reparation to God Almighty for her sin. But she owed a reparation, also, to those with whom she lived. She owed a reparation to the Protestant servants to whom she had given so fearful an example, for however they might laugh at her religion, they knew well how she ought to have practiced it.

She owed reparation to her master, and, above all, she felt that she could best repair the sin against her mistress by devoting herself, heart and soul, to the little baby, Rosaline, and, with her master's permission, she took entire charge of the child.

Mr. Maxwell did not concern himself, as she grew older, as to what religion she was taught, or, indeed, as to whether she was taught any religion. If she looked well and seemed happy, that was all he asked.

The question came before him one day, when he found that it was quite time that she should have some regular instruction. Naturally he spoke to Kathleen on the subject, and at her earnest entreaties, the little one was sent to a convent school.

Such an instance of liberality was far rarer then than it is now, when so many non-Catholic Americans are glad to take advantage of the superior education given in our Catholic convents.

The convents of America have, indeed, distinguished themselves in that matter before the whole world. May they prosper, and continue their divine work.

Kathleen had believed it to be her duty to remain in Mr. Maxwell's family until her little charge had made her first communion, and until she felt assured that her service was no longer needed. Then she obtained her heart's desire, and she is even now a devoted and faithful lay sister in the very convent where little Rosaline was educated.

But we have left the gentlemen too long conversing unnoticed. The question of a voyage to Europe was soon decided, and every preparation made with that expedition which wealth can always insure.

Rosaline remained in charge of the nuns—a bright, joyous, amiable child, and with a promise of being as beautiful as she was good.

CHAPTER VII.

THADE'S CHOICE.

Forevermore she hears us cry,
And helps in every misery.

"Oh, Mother of God ! Mother of God ! Mother of God !"
It was the cry of poor Thade's broken heart, when his grief
found utterance. What was he to do? Where was he to go?
Certainly, he said to himself, he would never again face his kind
friends; and where was he to look for help and shelter?

He had the firm trust in and the fervent devotion to the Mother
of Jesus which has ever been the characteristic of the Irish heart.
Young as he was, he said his rosary every night, and when was
any one ever forsaken who trusted to the powerful intercession of
our Blessed Lady?

It was a mere mechanical cry, when he moaned out his prayer,
"Mother of God ! Mother of God !" But if human mothers are
so full of love—if their hearts are so easily touched when they
hear the least cry from the lips of their children—how much more
quickly does the Divine Mother hear us, her poor children, for
whom she suffered such long hours of agony at the foot of the
cross of Jesus.

As Thade passed out of the church, his foot stumbled over what
seemed a small parcel.* He stooped down carelessly to pick it
up, but his mind was too absorbed in his grief to pay much attention, for the moment, to anything.

He held it in his hand for a second or two, doubtful whether

---

* A fact, and what follows also happened exactly as it is told.

he should throw it again on the ground, or leave it on a bench for the owner. A moment more, and it flashed on him that he had a pocket-book in his hand.

A purse!

A moment more, and he had ascertained that it was well filled with gold, and a large sum of money in bank-notes.

Here, indeed, was good fortune.

In a moment the boy was himself again. Surely, he thought, the Blessed Virgin herself had put this in his way. Now he could provide for himself. He would go to Dublin, he would go to America, he would make his fortune somewhere and somehow. At all events, he was safe from the terror and dread of going back to his master.

His good fortune almost stunned him for the moment, but thought is quick. How many things he had settled in his own mind, and acted over in his imagination in a few minutes.

But the one great thought was the overwhelming joy that he could now provide for himself.

We must do Thade the justice to say that it was not fear of punishment which made him so desirous to escape. He was too brave and manly a boy to wish to shirk a punishment which he knew he well deserved, as we have said. To his fine and noble nature, the shame and disgrace of having acted so badly toward those to whom he owed so much, was far more terrible than any chastisement which could be inflicted on him. He would, he thought, never see them again, until he could show them how truly he had repented—until he had made a name for himself in some way.

Poor boy! he little knew how difficult it would be to get name and fame; but youth is happily sanguine.

They should be proud of him when they would see him next. And he would buy the most magnificent horse for Mr. Tom. I am not sure that he had not decided on jewels and silks for Miss Kate.

Poor Thade! nay, rather let us say, rich Thade. Rich in his own generous, unselfish Irish heart. Better be Thade giving imaginary presents to those he loved, which he most certainly would have made real if he could, than your miserly boy, who thinks only of himself and his own selfish interests.

As he left the church porch, he began to hum a Litany of the Blessed Virgin softly to himself.

He turned to take a last look at the familiar spot, and to make a last reverence to the large and beautiful statue of our Blessed Lady outside the church.

But what has happened?

What change is this? Thade has ceased his joyous melody. He turns pale as death; a cold sweat bursts out on his fine, open forehead; he trembles in every limb.

"My God!" he mutters, in accents of alarm and horror; "I was near being a thief."

Never *that*, Thade, boy, whatever harm you may do.

A thief! The very thought was terrible.

As he turned and looked at the Mother of Jesus; she, too, looked at him—one long, tender, reproachful glance.

In one moment he realized his danger. He saw the peril from which he had been saved.

The money was not his own, and, at any cost, it must be returned to the owner.

Thade flew home. The fear of being tempted to sin if he kept the money a moment longer in his possession far outweighed the lesser fear.

He never even thought of what would be said to him, nor did he even for a moment consider that he was performing an act of virtue.

As he came near the house his courage cooled a little, but his determination, happily, never faltered for a moment.

Whom was he to speak to? How could he dare show his face to any of the family?

Mr. O'Grady's garden was divided from that of his neighbor by a close, thick hedge, which, however, was high enough to divide, but not too high for verbal communication. Thade remembered this, and went to the servant, whom he knew very well. She had heard his trouble, and pitied him sincerely, for Thade was a general favorite.

He told her his story, and that all he wanted was to get one word with Miss Kate, and then he would run off again.

This was easily managed.

Kate came to the hedge, and Thade cried out eagerly, "Oh, Miss Kate, Miss Kate, I've found some money; for God's sake take it," and he pushed the pocket-book into her hand, and prepared to run away.

But he could not resist the old associations of obedience and affection, and when Kate called him back eagerly, he returned.

"What is this, Thade? Come to me. I assure you my father was as anxious as any of us for your return."

"Oh, Miss Kate, sure I could never look one of you in the face again—you that reared me and cared for me all my life, and for me to go and kill Mr. Tom's horse, that I'd have died for any day."

It certainly was not quite clear whether Thade would have died for Tom, or the horse, or both; but Kate knew that his intentions, however wrongly expressed, were genuine, and she believed that he would have died willingly any day in his master's service.

"But what is this about the purse? Where did you get it? Where did it come from?"

"Well, Miss Kate, sure I thought the Blessed Virgin sent it to me to help me out of all my troubles, and I was just going to run away with it, and go to the devil entirely, when she just gave me one look, and sure that was enough."

"But," exclaimed Kate in amazement, "where did you see the Blessed Virgin, Thade?" She was, indeed, far too much astonished to question his assertions very carefully.

"Is it where I saw the Blessed Mother of God? Sure it was *just where she is*, outside the church, there; and she looked at me so sorrowful like."

"Well, but where did you get the purse?" replied Kate, who did not feel disposed to contest Thade's statement.

"You see, Miss Kate, I ran to the church and hid myself

there, for I was just dead with shame for what I had done, and I think I was praying all the time to the Blessed Virgin unknownst to me, and when it got quite dark I had to come away, and fell over that purse; and I said to myself, 'Glory be to God, Thade, you can go to America, or London, or anywhere now, and make your fortune, and not come home till you'll be a credit to them all.' And I was just off, when I looked back to bid the Blessed Virgin good-bye—on the statue, you mind, outside the door—and she just looked at me, Miss Kate, like you might do if I was doing wrong, and all in a moment *I knew what it was*, glory be to God! It was the same as if she said, 'Thade, you're a thief if you take that purse, and I'm sorry for you;' and sure I would not have *her* sorry for me, that is the joy of heaven, and shed more tears for us than all the world put together, except her blessed Son!"

"Thank God, Thade, you are not a thief," replied Kate. She was deeply touched by the boy's simple narrative, and did not doubt he had indeed received some miraculous grace in his hour of need.

"I will take the purse to my father," she continued. "He will know best what to do with it. He will be pleased with your honesty; and believe me, Thade, we will none of us ever reproach you with what has happened. It was an accident; but do, dear boy, remember that the fault of disobedience would have been equally great, even had no accident happened. It may have been a great mercy for you to have got such a lesson, hard as it seems, at the beginning of your life."

Kate was no hand at "preaching," and so she said no more; but her holy life was the best sermon she could have given to any one.

"I can let you into the stable, and no one will see you there to-night. To-morrow my father will tell you what to do."

Thade complied very cheerfully with the directions of his young mistress. He knew very well that he might travel far and wide before he would find such a home, and such good and true friends.

He was sobered and saddened, but he was sobered and saddened the right way; not with the depression of self-love, but
with the noble and invigorating sadness of holy fear.

Before he lay down to sleep that night—yes, before he even
tasted the good supper which Kate had brought him, guessing
that he had been fasting all day—he knelt down and thanked
God for all His mercies to him; and when he had satisfied his
hunger, he said his Rosary with fervent and honest devotion, and
made a resolution, which he faithfully kept, that for the rest of
his life he would be obedient to his superiors, and more than
ever devout to his Mother Mary.

CHAPTER VIII.

"THE BOY'S HONEST, AFTER ALL."

An honest heart, that never liked a fraud,
Nor gave deceit from out his clear blue eye.

"See what Thade's brought, father!" exclaimed Kate, as she entered the room where Mr. O'Grady sat, looking as if he had never stirred since morning, for he was occupied, as he had been then, with a newspaper.

Kate knew by long experience that the straightforward way was the best way with her hot-tempered but excellent father.

"A purse! So well filled, too. Where did you get it?"

Kate told him the story simply, as Thade had told her.

"Humph! Belongs to some tourist, I suppose. Well, the boy's honest, after all."

"Father!"

"Oh, just like you women. You think any one you like is right."

Kate was too wise to offer any contradiction. Mr. O'Grady was looking really pleased, but, man-like, he would not give his womankind the satisfaction of hearing any expressions of his satisfaction.

"That young scoundrel has given trouble enough for one day, and now to go and find this purse. Are you sure he didn't steal it?"

"You dear old dad!"

"Want to get at the soft side of me, eh? I see. I suppose you've cried over that boy, and killed the fatted calf for him.

Shouldn't wonder if you had a hot supper dressed for him on purpose."

"I gave him some bread and milk, and told him to go and sleep in the stable, and that you would see him in the morning."

"Did you tell him I would see him with a horse-whip? No, of course you didn't. I have a great mind to—"

But what Mr. O'Grady's mind was inclined to, remains unknown.

"Hallo, Tom, here's that boy of yours come home with a purse of gold that he's found or stolen."

"Faith, sir, I wish I'd find one."

Tom was always short of cash. Was there ever a boy yet who had all he desired?

"I suppose, now, I must go to the police, and go round to all the hotels and give notice, or we'll have that boy taken up and put in jail on suspicion, if any one finds out what he's got."

"Can't you write, father?"

Kate had been occupying herself during this conversation in providing pens and paper; but Mr. O'Grady would not condescend to notice her.

Men have their grievances, as well as women; and we must do them the justice to say that when they have, they generally do their best to make them known.

A note was presently dispatched to the police and to the hotels, Mr. O'Grady insisting on writing all himself, though Tom and Kate were quite willing to help him. But if he permitted them, how could he make himself out a martyr to Thade's sins "and vicious propensity for finding purses"?

Mr. O'Grady wrote to the police, and the writing ran thus:

"SIR:—A lad in my employment has found a purse in the Catholic Church, late last night. It is at present in my possession, and will be restored to the owner on his making personal application for it, and describing purse and contents."

"There they are!" exclaimed Tom, as, on the following morning, the O'Gradys sat at breakfast.

"Who and where?" inquired Mr. O'Grady, not without a

slight gleam of malice. He was fond of having a hit at Tom's random speeches.

"Who—party unknown, sir, but suspect their errand is the purse; where—well, I should say at the hall-door by this time."

A fact sufficiently patent and self-evident, since a loud ring was heard at that very moment.

A few minutes more, and the courteous and gentlemanly host of the Lake Hotel was introducing two American gentlemen "of fortune and distinction" to the O'Grady family.

"We have ventured to intrude on you early, sir," observed the elder of the two gentlemen, who had just presented his card, and who was a New York friend to whom the reader has been already introduced—the father of the pretty Rosaline.

Mr. O'Grady assured his visitors that no apology was necessary—tourists were privileged.

A few minutes served to convince all parties that there had been no mistake, and that no fraud or deception was intended. Mr. Maxwell stated the amount of money which was contained in the purse, and it was found intact. His initials, too, were engraved on it, so there could be no doubt.

"But where," asked his companion, Mr. Hillman, "is the boy who has found this valuable purse? He must be well rewarded for his honesty."

Thade was summoned to the parlor, much to his dismay; and, much to the amazement of the gentlemen, he fell on his knees when he entered, more like a culprit than one who was about to receive a reward.

But the honest, open face certainly did not suggest any mistrust.

"O sir, O master, if you'll forgive me—"

The story of Thade's misadventure was soon told, and both gentlemen were deeply interested.

His appearance, his manner and his address were greatly in his favor, and he had an air of refinement beyond his station— partly the result of natural gifts, and partly a consequence of the association with superiors who, while they did not seek to raise him above his position, had certainly treated him with more than ordinary familiarity.

"Well, my boy," said Mr. Maxwell, "I am sure your master will forgive you freely. I will ask it as a personal favor to myself;" and, handing him a bank note of some value, "here is what I hope will help to set you up in an honest and humble career, and I will send you a further remittance from New York from time to time."

But, to the surprise of both gentlemen, Thade firmly but courteously refused the proffered reward.

"Is it to pay me for being honest and for pleasing the Blessed Virgin? Oh, no, sir. Indeed, I am grateful to you both, gentlemen," he said, with the ready tact of his nature when he saw that his refusal of the gift had given pain; "but I could not take it. If the master will forgive me and trust me again—and he shall never, never repent it—that is all that I'll take from any one, and God knows it's more than I deserve."

Thade was not to be shaken in his resolution, and the two gentlemen went away with a new view of the Irish character, and certainly more impressed than they could well express.

"A noble boy," exclaimed Mr. Maxwell, as they drove back to the hotel to prepare for a day's pleasure.

Mr. Hillman said nothing, but it was quite evident that he was deeply absorbed in thought during the remainder of the day.

CHAPTER IX.

THADE FINDS NEW FRIENDS.

"I have no son, Mr. O'Grady; my wife died immediately after the birth of our little girl. We were very deeply attached to one another, and I never even thought of marrying again."

"But you are still a young man; you may change your mind."

"Well, sir, I believe that I shall not change my mind, but, as you say, it is possible. I wish to adopt Thade, and I want some one who will have my interest at heart in my business. When my girl is a little older, I will travel with her in Europe for several years. I have trustworthy clerks; but you know, sir, what a difference it makes to any business to have one whose heart is devoted to your interests, as well as his head."

"I will not stand in Thade's way for a moment," replied Mr. O'Grady. "He must be the person to decide. He is quite old enough. But you had better hear more of his history before you see him."

Mr. Maxwell listened with the attentive consideration of a man who knows the subject spoken of to be one of grave importance.

"And do you tell me, sir," he exclaimed, in amazement, "that there are people in this country who will deliberately try to buy and sell a man's religion in this way!"

"It is, unfortunately, too true. No doubt some of the Protestants who act thus think that they are influenced by good motives; but, for a great majority, there is every reason to believe that the whole affair is a mere traffic in souls—a traffic by which they benefit their temporal interests, which is their only concern. If you knew something of our people, and if you had been, as I have been, an eye-witness of their courage and constancy under trial, you would at least believe that they had a faith which taught them to do and suffer as no man could suffer or act for a mere opinion."

"You will, perhaps, be surprised to hear that, though I do not profess your religion myself, I have allowed my little girl to be brought up a Catholic, and that she is at present being educated in a convent school."

Mr. O'Grady was surprised, but the knowledge of this circumstance removed what he felt to be one great objection to parting with Thade.

He knew very well that those who are proof against adversity are not always proof against prosperity—that there was no more dangerous temptation to the young than sudden advancement in their wordly prospects; and much as he would desire to see Thade advanced in life, he certainly would not desire that this advancement should be purchased by the sacrifice of a single principle.

Mr. Maxwell's friend was listening to this assurance with an indifference which was wholly assumed, to hide the deepest feeling.

"Well," he said, "gentlemen, I guess Thade had better settle the proposal for himself."

Thade was summoned, looking, certainly, very much brighter than on the preceding day.

"Thade," said Mr. O'Grady, "here is an offer for you. Mr. Maxwell proposes to take you back with him to New York; to give you the education of a gentleman, and put you in a position which you can certainly never expect to hold in this country. I think I can promise for him that he will never seek to interfere with your religion. It is for you to decide this important point. What do you say?"

Thade was fairly bewildered, as well he might be. For a few moments he stared in blank amazement at the two gentlemen. Then he seemed suddenly to realize the offer that had been made to him.

"Is it to leave you, and Mr. Tom, and Brian Boru, and Miss Kate?"

Mr. O'Grady smiled at the incongruous collection of the objects of his affection.

"Well, something like it, Thade. I'm afraid I'm rather old to travel now, and, you see, Mr. Maxwell could not adopt us all."

"Is it to go out of it, and never see one of you again, sir?"

"Well, you might see some of us again, Thade. But this is a serious matter."

"I think you will have no cause to regret it, if you come with me, Thade. I have a large business in New York, and I have no son of my own to take any of the care from me. I will have you educated as if you were my own child, and when you are old enough, I will place you in a confidential position in my bank. I told you, boy, that I believe you to be thoroughly upright and honest, and that this is the great consideration which induces me to make you this offer."

Thade's eyes were filling fast with tears. He began clearly to understand the matter. Naturally, he wished to advance himself, and he was old enough to have some idea of the importance and value of the offer which was made to him. But his affections were strong. He had that happy disregard of consequences and indifference to pecuniary advantage which one so often sees in our people, and which one scarcely knows whether to admire or deplore.

But affection seemed destined to carry the day. He flung himself at his master's feet in a passion of tears.

"I'll never leave you, sir—never!"

But Mr. O'Grady was too well aware of the consequences involved in this decision to allow him to make it thus. He asked the gentlemen to leave Thade an hour, to think the matter over quietly. With this request they willingly complied, and, on their return, Thade, following the advice of Mr. O'Grady and of Miss Kate, decided gratefully to accept the splendid position he was offered.

He was at once taken away to procure an outfit; and when he was presented to his former master, attired in his new clothing, no one could deny that, in appearance at least, he was no disgrace to the station in life which Providence had now assigned him.

CHAPTER X.

TEN YEARS LATER.

Oh, Ireland, mother Ireland,
My heart still turns to thee,
And longs and pines with constant love,
Thy holy shores to see.

"And so, my darling, the wedding-day is fixed, and you are going to my dear old country, my own old Ireland."

Something like a tear glistened in the great eye of the good lay sister. Ever since the time of St. Colomba, and before it, a passionate love of Ireland has been the born heritage of the Celt.

The heaviest penance that could be put upon the erring saint was that he should never see Ireland again, and, as the chronicler tells us, he came and went with a sere cloth over his eyes and a sod of the land of Atta under his feet, so that when duty called him to his beloved Erin, he might fulfill his penance—so that he might neither see nor touch the earth of his native country.

Kathleen had now been a nun for some years, but she did not lose her love of Ireland. Perhaps the hardest part of her self-imposed penance had been to renounce all hope of seeing motherland again. If the desire to do so still remained, it only remained as a new source of penance, sacrifice and love.

She had chosen the name of Magdalen, as one which she believed specially suitable to her sorrow and her love. She had sinned much indeed, for she had sinned against light and knowledge and abundant grace. But her repentance was deep and most truly sincere. Her history was known only to her superioress; but it was noticed by all that she lived a life of great austerity—not in great things, this was not permitted by her Holy Rule—but she practiced to the full that higher, far more difficult austerity—the mortification of every sense, faculty and desire in her daily life; and it was also noticed that she was specially devoted to the interest of young girls who were preparing for service; that she had eloquent and abundant words for them, however reticent she might be towards others, and that she would entreat them, with words of most impressive earnestness, to give good example, and to strengthen themselves for their duties by frequent attendance at the sacraments, and to take care lest at any time they should be guilty of the spiritual murder of those with whom they associated, by giving bad example, or prove themselves unworthy of their glorious heritage of faith.

We have no more to say now of Sister Mary Magdalen, save that she lived long to do her work of reparation and penance, and that she did it well and faithfully.

It was to her dear child, Rosaline, she spoke. Rosaline, whom she loved as tenderly as ever mother loved child, and with an affection little less than maternal.

"Mr. O'Halloran is worthy of your choice, and I thank God that you are to be united to one of your own faith and one of my country."

"It is a great happiness, at least," replied gentle Rosaline, "that every one is so pleased."

The dear child, for she was still little more, had given the affections of her young heart to Thade. Her aristocratic family had chaffed her not a little upon her choice. He was "Irish" and a Roman Catholic, and no one knew anything about his family, though, in truth, his descent might have been traced up to a higher rank than that of any of his despisers, however humble the circumstances of his birth had been; and the position in Mr. Maxwell's bank, to which he had been raised by his honesty and his talent, could not fail to command respect in a country where business ability is held in special honor, and where intellect takes rank as nature's patent of nobility.

"But I have news for you, sister," said Rosaline, when all particulars of the wedding and the wedding tour had been fully discussed. "You know we have not seen papa's old friend, Mr. Hillman, since he was ordained deacon. We heard from him to-day, and he sent me this," she said, producing an exquisitely-bound missal, his wedding gift. "He is to be ordained priest the Sunday after my wedding day."

Sister Mary Magdalen ejaculated a heart-felt "Thank God," and well she might.

And all this came of Tim O'Halloran's choice.

Thade's conduct, on the occasion of his first introduction to his patron, so soon to be his father-in-law, had made a very deep impression on this gentleman. He said very little; in fact, he affected to treat the whole affair with good-natured contempt; but he reflected none the less deeply. He felt that there must be something in a faith which could lead a boy to such practical honesty from such high motives. He learned that the Irish, even when uneducated, were a people of great natural ability; that they were very far from deserving the contempt which the ignorant too often bestowed on them. Several years' experience of Thade—his steadiness in business, his admirable conduct in prosperity, his quiet, patient religion—each and all made a deep and blessed impression.

Then Mr. Hillman began to ask himself what *he* was living for, and what was his life likely to be worth hereafter. He had independent means; he could choose, without let or hindrance, his own future career; and having been received into the Holy Catholic Church, he chose the humble, lowly, laborious, self-denying life of a Catholic priest.

Little did the good farmer, whose death-bed scene forms the opening chapter of our tale, ever imagine the many happy results which would follow from his glorious fidelity to his faith. Little did he imagine how God would reward, and how many would live to bless

TIM. O'HALLORAN'S CHOICE.

www.ingramcontent.com/pod-product-compliance
Lightning Source LLC
Chambersburg PA
CBHW032150010726
47493CB00008BA/2650